NICARAGUA
STRUGGLING WITH CHANGE

DISCOVERING our HERITAGE

by Faith Adams

DILLON PRESS, INC.
Minneapolis, Minnesota 55415

The photographs are reproduced through the courtesy of Faith Adams, Ione Adams, Dick Bancroft, Susan Bradford, Bill Cameron, Casa Oscar Romero, Gerald Dillon, Kevin Hartigan, and Sandy Pappas.

Library of Congress Cataloging in Publication Data

Adams, Faith.
  Nicaragua : struggling with change.

  (Discovering our heritage)
  Bibliography: p.
  Includes index.
  Summary: Discusses the history and culture of the Nicaraguan people and contemporary life in this country torn apart by conflicting forces in the twentieth century.
  1. Nicaragua—Juvenile literature. [1. Nicaragua—Juvenile literature. [1. Nicaragua] I. Title. II. Series.
F1523.2.A33   1987   972.85   86-11608
ISBN 0-87518-340-5

Dillon Press, Inc., 242 Portland Avenue South
Minneapolis, Minnesota 55415

Printed in the United States of America
1 2 3 4 5 6 7 8 9 10 96 95 94 93 92 91 90 89 88 87

Contents

Fast Facts About Nicaragua

Official Name: *República de Nicaragua* ("Republic of Nicaragua").

Capital: Managua.

Location: Central America; Honduras lies to the north, Costa Rica lies to the south, the Pacific Ocean lies to the west, and the Atlantic Ocean forms the coastline to the east.

Area: 50,193 square miles (130,000 square kilometers) *Greatest Distances*: north-south—293 miles (472 kilometers); east-west—297 miles (478 kilometers) *Coastlines*: Pacific—215 miles (346 kilometers); Caribbean—297 miles (478 kilometers).

Elevation: *Highest*—8,000 feet (2,438 meters) above sea level in the Cordillera Isabella; *Lowest*—sea level.

Population: 3,145,000 (1986 estimate); *Distribution*—Urban—57%, Rural—43%; *Density*—62 persons per square mile (24 per square kilometer).

Form of Government: Democratic republic. Elections based on proportional representation for president, vice president, and a 96-member national assembly were held in 1984. A constitution is being drafted to replace the 1974 constitution, which was abandoned in 1979.

Important Products: *Agriculture*—bananas, beans, beef cattle, coffee, corn, cotton, rice, sesame, sugar cane. *Manufacturing*—clothing and textiles, processed foods and beverages.

Basic Unit of Money: Córdoba.

Major Languages: Spanish. English and the Indian languages Miskito, Sumo, and Rama are spoken on the Atlantic coast.

Major Religion: Roman Catholic; many people on the Atlantic coast are Protestants.

Flag: Three horizontal stripes in blue, white, and blue.

National Anthem: *Himno Nacional de Nicaragua* ("National Hymn of Nicaragua").

Major Holidays: New Year's Day—January 1; Holy Thursday; Good Friday; Labor Day—May 1; Anniversary of the Sandinista Revolution—July 19; Battle of San Jacinto—September 14; Independence Day—September 15; Purísima—December 7; Christmas Day—December 25.

1. A Nation at War

Nicaragua is a country in the midst of change. Although it is an old country in history and customs, it is a country of young people and new ideas. Half of the people in Nicaragua are less than fifteen years old. In the capital, Managua, new parks and libraries for these young people are being built next to the ruins of buildings from the earthquake that destroyed most of the city in 1972.

In the countryside, farmers plant corn and beans at new government-run farms and older private farms. The farmers are planting land that had become overgrown with weeds while the Nicaraguan people fought in a civil war during the late 1970s.

Today another war is being fought in Nicaragua. Soldiers called *contras*, or counterrevolutionaries, are fighting against the Nicaraguan government. The war affects the lives of people throughout the country. For some it means the deaths of family members, while for others it means shortages of food and other needs. For everyone it means learning to live with constant change.

A Central American Nation

Nicaragua is the largest country in Central America, which is located between Mexico and South Amer-

Like these young people, half of the people in Nicaragua are less than fifteen years old.

ica. Central America is made up of a long, narrow chain of seven countries. Guatemala and Belize lie next to the southern border of Mexico. Honduras and El Salvador are next in the chain, followed by Nicaragua, Costa Rica, and Panama. Nicaragua is six times larger than El Salvador, the smallest Central American country.

The Caribbean Sea borders Nicaragua on the east, and the Pacific Ocean lies to the west. Honduras borders Nicaragua on the north. To the south, across the San Juan River and Lake Nicaragua, is Costa Rica.

Nicaragua has a long coast on the Atlantic Ocean and a shorter coast on the Pacific side. The eastern part of the country, called either *Costa Atlántica ("Atlantic Coast")* or *Costa Miskito* ("Miskito Coast"), is very different from the west. Three out of four Nicaraguans live in the western part of the country, on the Pacific side. In the middle of Nicaragua lies a large, nearly unpopulated area which separates the two coasts. Most Nicaraguans never travel through this middle section and visit the other coast. In fact, few roads link the Atlantic coast area to western Nicaragua. Boat and plane travel are the main means of transportation. It is almost as if Nicaragua is made up of two different countries.

Most people on the Pacific side are *mestizos* of mixed Spanish and Indian ancestry. These people inherited many of their traditions from the Spaniards who settled in Nicaragua four hundred years ago. They speak Spanish and attend the Roman Catholic church. Yet some of their traditions are those of their Indian ancestors. Nicaraguans in this part of the country eat beans and corn tortillas every day, just as their Indian ancestors did hundreds of years ago. Most Nicaraguans

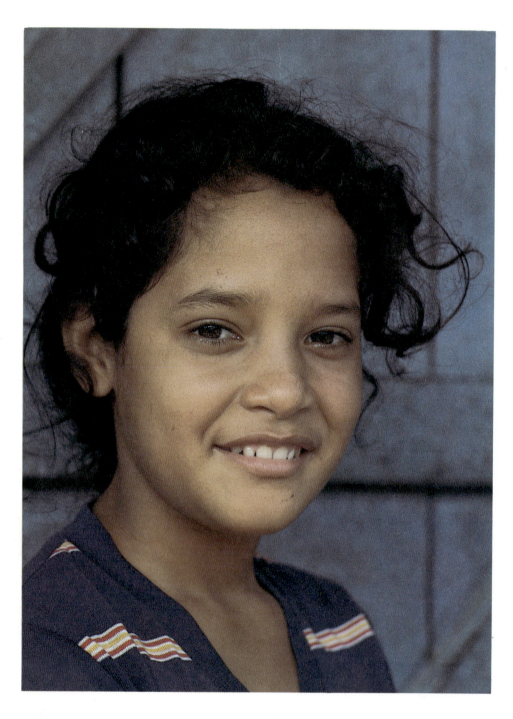

This young woman, like most Nicaraguans, is a mestizo of mixed Spanish and Indian ancestry.

A Sumo woman on the Atlantic coast. The Sumo, Rama, and Miskito Indians are native to Nicaragua.

are small farmers, just as the Indians were. But rather than growing mainly corn, they now also raise coffee, cotton, and sugar cane.

Four main groups of people live along the Atlantic coast: the Miskito, Rama, and Sumo Indians, who are native to Nicaragua, and the Garifunos, who are blacks originally from Africa. The Garifunos speak English, and each Indian group has its own Indian language. Miskito is the most commonly spoken language on the Atlantic coast. Many of the houses in the Atlantic coast region are built on stilts to protect people from floods

during heavy rains and from the snakes and spiders that live here. Nicaraguans in the Atlantic area eat seafood and coconut bread, among other things, because both are abundant on the coast.

Although Nicaragua is large in land area (about the size of the state of Wisconsin), it has a small population compared with other Central American countries. Fewer people—about three million—live in Nicaragua than in the much smaller El Salvador. That makes it the most thinly populated country in Central America. Nearly half of its people, though, live in Managua, León, and other large cities in western Nicaragua.

A Long and Sad History

The word *Nicaragua* comes from *Nicarao*, which was the name of an Indian chief and his tribe who lived near Lake Nicaragua at the time the Spanish conquerors came to the region. Some language experts believe that Nicaragua means "here near the lake."

The people of Nicaragua have had a long and oftentimes sad history. The Spaniards who came to this region in the early 1500s forced the Indians to change their way of life. The changes were sudden, often harsh, and as a result many Indians died.

In the 1800s and 1900s the Nicaraguan people— who were now mostly mestizo, part Spanish and part

A Garifuno man, whose ancestors came originally from Africa.

Indian—were ruled by a series of dictators. These dictators had all of the power in Nicaragua. One family that ruled the country for more than forty years—the Somozas—kept a group of soldiers called the National Guard. The National Guard was responsible for torturing, and sometimes killing, people who were opposed to the government in power.

In 1979 the people of Nicaragua, led by a group called the Sandinistas, won a bitter war against Anastasio Somoza Debayle, the last Nicaraguan dictator. Buildings throughout the country still show much damage as a result of the war. Forty thousand people died in the struggle. During Somoza's rule, he kept most of the nation's wealth for himself and a few friends.

The revolutionary group now in power—the Sandinistas—is changing the lives of the people. Its goal is to make life better for the many thousands of poor Nicaraguans by providing health care, education, food, and housing. The process is long and slow, for most Nicaraguans are still poor. And yet, the government has introduced a number of important new social programs.

Not everyone in Nicaragua agrees with the way the Sandinistas are running the country. Some of them have armed themselves and fight against the Sandinista army. These armed guerrillas—the contras—don't believe the Sandinistas should be in power. They claim that the Sandinistas are dangerous Communists who are taking away the rights and freedoms of the Nicaraguan people. The contras are fighting a guerrilla war. That means they fight in small bands and sneak through the countryside to take their enemy by surprise.

The contra war is fought mostly along Nicaragua's long border with Honduras. People who live in the border areas are tired of war and fear for their lives. They sometimes leave the war zone where they live and travel to a city just to get away from the fighting for a time. Now and then groups of children from the war zone are taken to stay in a safe place, too.

A Confusing Capital

Though most Nicaraguans live in rural areas, more and more of them are moving to cities, especially to Managua. The destruction and danger of the contra war zone make it difficult for people to make a living in the war zones. People also move to cities in hopes of getting better jobs. Managua, Nicaragua's largest city, sprawls along the southwest shore of Lake Managua. In 1979 Managua was home to 600,000 people. Today it has a population of more than 900,000 and continues to grow rapidly.

Downtown Managua is a confusing place. Almost all of the buildings were destroyed in the earthquake

Cows graze among overgrown grass and weeds where downtown Managua stood before the 1972 earthquake.

that shook the city in 1972. Five thousand people died in the earthquake. In place of downtown buildings, there are now several blocks of overgrown grass and weeds where cows sometimes graze. Buses and taxis drive by cows right next to the busy street.

The 1972 earthquake is not the only disaster that Managua has suffered. The city has had a series of fires and earthquakes, which have meant rebuilding the city time and again. In 1951 a terrible earthquake and resulting fire all but destroyed Managua. Thousands of people lost their lives and homes.

This part of Nicaragua lies within the Ring of Fire, a narrow belt that goes along the edges of the continents and the islands surrounding the Pacific Ocean. The land lying under the Ring of Fire has the most intense earthquake and volcanic activity in the world.

In Managua today, the National Palace and cathedral are two of the few colonial buildings still standing. As a result of the earthquake, the cathedral has four walls but no roof. Weeds and grass have grown up through the floor. Because the center of the city is located on a fault line where earthquakes are likely to occur again, the government has decided to build recreational facilities and parks in the old center of Managua instead of tall buildings which could be destroyed.

Locating places in Managua is all the more difficult because there are no street names. Directions to someone's house are very simple: the *barrio* ("neighborhood") name and the house number are the only instructions given. The directions may be simple, but finding the house is usually not quite so simple! People in Managua give tips by naming a nearby landmark, such as a church or restaurant. They also give directions according to natural landmarks. For instance, *lago* ("lake") is the direction used instead of north. *Arriba* ("up") means east. *Montaña* ("mountain") means south, and west is *abajo* ("down"). That way, if you can see the lake, you will know which direction north is.

Although it looks abandoned in some places, Managua can be very beautiful, too. The whole city is visible from the top of *Loma de Tiscapa* ("Tiscapa Hill"). From the top of this hill, the Tiscapa Lagoon below sparkles like a melted jewel. The Tiscapa Lagoon is a shallow lake which has filled a big hole once made by an enormous volcano.

Volcanoes, Cotton Fields, and Beaches

There are several lagoons in Managua and the surrounding area, and some have been created by volcanic activity. Of the more than twenty-seven volcanoes that rise along the Pacific Ocean, eight are active. The soil near the volcanoes has been enriched by volcanic ash. It makes fertile ground for the coffee, cotton, and sugar cane grown in these areas.

Between Managua and the city of León rises a volcano named Momotombo. Momotombo dominates the skyline of Lake Managua and on a clear day creates a reflection in the water. A very high, perfectly cone-shaped volcano, its summit is sometimes lost in the clouds.

Viewed from the top of Tiscapa Hill, the Tiscapa Lagoon below sparkles like a melted jewel.

Momotombo is located halfway between Managua and León, the second largest city in Nicaragua. León has an ancient air about it. Narrow streets wind between low adobe houses topped with red-tiled roofs. The largest cathedral in Central America was built in León by mistake. The Spanish government, which paid for the building, had intended the cathedral to be built in Peru!

León is surrounded by dry, flat plains planted with cotton. The workers who harvest cotton work long, hot, tiring days. When the sun is directly above, between 10:00 A.M. and 2:00 P.M., you can see no shadows from your body. The heat is so intense that it feels as though there is not even a shadow under your feet! The sun rises and sets quickly in Nicaragua because it is near the equator. Dawn and dusk don't last long at all. The sun rises between 5:00 and 5:30, and by 7:30 it shines from halfway up in the sky.

Not far from León are beautiful, sandy beaches. Some of them have resorts that are popular with people from Nicaragua's cities. At the beach town of Poneloya, swimmers have to be very careful. The undertow, a current of water moving beneath and in a different direction from the surface water, is so strong that it knocks swimmers over and pulls them into deep water. Many people have died swimming here. Most visitors play in the shallow water and enjoy the feel of the undertow as it goes swirling by.

Life by the "Great Lake"

On the drive south from Managua is a lake even bigger than Lake Managua. It is Lake Nicaragua, the biggest lake in the Western Hemisphere between Lake Michigan in the United States and Lake Titicaca in

A house stands among graceful palm trees on one of the inhabited islands in Lake Nicaragua.

Peru. Lake Nicaragua, also known as the *Gran Lago* ("Great Lake"), is about 103 miles (165 kilometers) long and 45 miles (72 kilometers) wide. There are more than 300 islands in the lake, most of them inhabited by people. There are even three volcanoes on these islands.

The children who live on these islands go by boat to get to the island that has the school. When they are old

enough, they learn to row a boat so they can get around
on their own. If their neighbor has a cow, they may row
to the next island to get milk. Some of the islands are so
small that there is just enough room for one family.

Lake Nicaragua is a freshwater lake full of saltwater
fish. There have even been some sharks in this lake!
Scientists believe that these saltwater fish ended up in
Lake Nicaragua because the lake was once part of a
huge ocean bay. The bay was closed off by a volcanic
eruption or an earthquake or both, trapping the fish.
Gradually, the waters of the lake became less salty, and
the fish adapted to the change in the water.

The city of Granada is located on the shore of Lake
Nicaragua. It is a grand city with many old colonial
buildings. Its stark white churches stand out against the
deep blue sky. Granada looks like a city in Spain, not
only because of the buildings but also because of the
people. There are many tall people with fair skin and
hair who look very much like their Spanish ancestors.

Masaya, a town near Granada, is known for handi-
crafts such as baskets and hammocks. Tobacco is grown
in the fields around Masaya. Nearby, the volcano Santi-
ago sends great billows of smoke into the air. The top of
the volcano can be reached by car. It is said that during
the years Somoza ruled Nicaragua, he would have his
enemies dropped into the mouth of the volcano from a
helicopter after they had been killed.

Weather and Seasons

Northern Nicaragua has fewer volcanoes and more mountains than the western part of the country. In the cattle-raising and coffee-growing areas of Matagalpa and Jinotega, the mountains appear rough and worn in some places and grand and beautiful in other places. The mountains have strange angles and shapes. One looks like a woman lying on her side and resting her head on her hand.

People from southern Nicaragua think that weather in Matagalpa is *bien fresco* ("nice and cool"). Here it is somewhat cooler and less humid than in León and Granada, but it is usually hot during the middle of the day. Women in Matagalpa sometimes carry umbrellas in order to protect their skin from the afternoon sun. Men wear straw hats which tie under the chin to keep the sun out of their eyes. It cools off at night here because of the high altitude.

In the western part of Nicaragua there are two seasons—the wet winter season and the dry summer season. The wet season lasts from May to November, and the dry season lasts from December to May. The dry season is the hotter of the two. The wet season is also hot, but a rain comes almost every day to cool things off for a while. The rain comes hard and without much warning. Though the sun may be shining in the morn-

ing, by mid-afternoon the rain comes down in sheets.

Eastern Nicaragua has no difference in the seasons—the weather is always hot and wet. Annual rainfall averages from 100 inches (254 centimeters) in the north to 300 inches (762 centimeters) in the south. The tropical climate along the Atlantic coast is the wettest in Central America. No wonder monkeys, alligators, and snakes live here. It's also the kind of weather that bananas need in order to grow. The Atlantic coast region produces bananas and good quality lumber.

Bluefields, named after the Dutch pirate Bleuwveldt, is the most important Caribbean port. Not far from Bluefields are the Corn Islands. These two small tropical islands are fringed with white coral and coconut trees. They are popular with tourists, especially those who scuba dive.

Though Nicaragua has rich natural resources, in the past most Nicaraguans who worked the land and harvested the resources were very poor. Peasants with no jobs had to seek jobs on large estates, where they were employed only three to six months a year and often earned less than a dollar a day. Most Nicaraguans are still poor farmers, but now many of them have a plot of their own land. Others work on government or privately owned farms for a better salary than they earned in the past. Throughout Nicaragua these poor people hope for a better life than they had before.

The city of Matagalpa nestles among the mountains of northern Nicaragua.

2. Poets, Priests, and Change

When you walk down a city street in Nicaragua, you can look into houses through open doorways and see families gathered around the television or the dinner table. Most people leave their front doors wide open when they are at home, throughout the day, and into the evening. People greet passersby with a nod and *"hola"* ("hello") or *adiós* ("good-bye").

Surrounded by People

Nicaraguans are accustomed to togetherness; they are surrounded by people most of the time. Houses are usually small and close together, and most have such thin walls that the neighbors can hear much of what goes on next door. They especially know when the baby next door cries in the middle of the night!

Buses and markets are often crowded with people. In the hot afternoons passengers riding home from work on the bus have to lean against each other to make room for more passengers. At the market shoppers must walk very carefully so they can find the produce they want to buy without running into too many other shoppers.

In public streets and private homes, city-dwelling Nicaraguans are surrounded by people most of the time.

A Nicaraguan family in the town of Masaya prepares to board a bus.

Nicaraguans are also accustomed to living without much privacy. Most households are large and made up of more than one family. Aunts or uncles and nieces or nephews often live with other relatives. When grandparents get old, they usually live with their families instead of living alone.

In most parts of Nicaragua, people greet friends and acquaintances warmly. Many Nicaraguans are open and friendly with strangers as well. Children walk up to strangers, especially foreigners, on the street and ask them all kinds of questions. *"¿Qué hora es?* ("What time is it?") *"¿Cuántos años tiene?"* ("How old are you?") Sometimes they ask because they want to know the answer to the question. At other times they are playing a game to find out if the foreigners speak Spanish.

Adults in Nicaragua are often curious about strangers and generous to them. On a long bus ride through the countryside, a Nicaraguan woman shares her bag of cookies with the foreign woman sitting next to her. A woman in Managua shares her home for three days with a couple of unexpected guests from another country.

In the war zones people are afraid to welcome strangers. They live under daily strain because of the contra war and don't know who they can trust. Sometimes their worries make them sad and quiet.

Arts for the People

Now and then the war zones are visited by groups of traveling actors. Alan Bolt, Nicaragua's most famous playwright, is also the director of the National Theater Workshop. The workshop is located on the outskirts of the city of Matagalpa. The actors from this workshop often split up and live in remote parts of the country to find out what problems people are facing. Then they return to their workshop and create a play based on

This street dance in Masaya is one expression of Nicaraguan culture.

these problems. When they travel around to perform the play, the people in the audience see themselves and their own problems in a way that has meaning for them. Often there is a lesson to be learned in the play.

Cultural activities, such as painting, poetry, dance, and theater, are very important in Nicaragua. Minister of Culture Ernesto Cardenal believes that the arts should be available to everyone, not just to those who can afford to pay for them. He also believes that people should learn to create art, music, and literature instead of just listening to them or looking at them. Cardenal

A mural of Nicaragua's history covers the wall along an entire city block in Managua.

says that everyone has a right to these expressions of culture, just as everyone has a right to food and clothing and housing. Nicaragua's three newspapers have responded by including a weekly section filled with poetry, drawings, and short stories. Cardenal wants to take art out of museums and put it outside for all to see.

Brightly painted murals cover walls of buildings throughout Nicaragua. A mural in Granada shows a woman carrying the blue and white Nicaraguan flag and walking beside a man carrying the red and black flag of the Sandinista party. A mural of Nicaragua's history covers the wall along an entire city block in Managua. Some art experts say that Nicaragua will soon become the world capital of mural art.

In order to bring the arts to everyone, the government has placed thirty-two centers for popular culture across the country. These centers offer poetry workshops and teach classes in folkdance, painting, and many other arts and crafts.

A Nation of Poets

Writing poetry is an everyday activity in Nicaragua. According to Nicaraguans, all Nicaraguans are poets! Nicaragua has produced more leading poets than any other country in Spanish America, even though most Nicaraguans could not read or write until recently. Peruvian writer Mario Vargas Llosa says that "Nicaraguans have a natural urge for poetry."

Half of the cabinet members in the government are poets. Minister of Culture Ernesto Cardenal is the best-known living writer in Nicaragua and probably the most widely read poet using the Spanish language today. He is a priest who founded a community named *Nuestra Señora de Solentiname* ("Our Lady of Solentiname") on a group of thirty-eight islands in the southern part of Lake Nicaragua. The community was originally intended to be a place for Christians to study their religion and examine their beliefs. It also became a community of artists, and is especially known for the fine painters who have worked there.

Much of Cardenal's poetry expresses the theme of love. In his early poetry, he deals with love of women. Later his poetry focuses on love of the tropics, the lakes, on everything that is Nicaragua. Eventually his poems center around love of God. Cardenal writes about the real things around us every day. He calls this *"exteriorismo,"* which comes from the Latin word *exterior.*

In Nicaragua a poet such as Ernesto Cardenal is sometimes called *"Poeta Cardenal"* ("Poet Cardenal") much as a doctor or priest is given a title. "Poet" isn't a formal or honorary title, but people may use it because they like to treat poets with great respect.

As a child, Cardenal read the poetry of Rubén Darío, who is considered to be Spanish America's greatest poet. Darío was born in 1867 in the town of Metapa in the northern province of Matagalpa. He left Nicaragua before he was twenty and after publishing one book of poems in Managua. Darío lived mainly in Chile and Argentina, working as a newspaper reporter and customs agent. His first important work was a collection of stories and poetry called *Azul* ("Blue"). He also published *Prosas Profanas* ("Profane Prose") and *Cantos de Vida y Esperanza* ("Songs of Life and Hope").

Darío is most famous for beginning what is known as the Modernist movement in literature. He started

The Rubén Darío Theater in Managua was named after Spanish America's greatest poet.

writing poetry with strong vowels and soft consonants and quit using the earlier Spanish style of poetry, which had soft, rhyming sounds.

Darío was influenced by French literature when he lived in France and served as Nicaraguan ambassador. In his old age he lived in León, where he was buried in the cathedral in 1916. His tomb is guarded by a statue of a lion. Each year, on Darío's birthday, poets and listeners gather at his birthplace to take part in a reading that lasts from dawn to dusk.

Music and a Giant Puppet

Music is another form of popular art in Nicaragua. Music is everywhere. Children sing songs they learn at school. While women make supper, they sing along with the music playing on the radio. People who can afford a stereo often play it at high volume all day long.

Cawibe and Dimensión Costeña are a couple of popular groups from the Atlantic coast region. They play reggae music that has an African origin and a slow, fluid beat. Praxis from western Nicaragua is a well-known jazz/rock band that plays music with a political message.

Nicaragua's best-known composer, Luis A. Delgadillo, wrote a wide variety of music. He composed sixteen symphonies and other music suitable for the Managua Chamber Orchestra. Another composer, Carlos Mejia Godoy, wrote political music such as the Sandinista anthem.

Because most Nicaraguan culture is Spanish, the ministry of culture wants to rediscover Indian ways and make people aware of their Indian background. In the Indian community of Subtiava, some Indian traditions

La Gigantona, *a huge puppet representing a woman, dances to the sound of drums.*

are still alive. Sometimes Subtiavans play drums, and *la Gigantona* ("The Giant One") dances to the sound of drums. The Gigantona is a huge puppet representing a woman. An adult fits under the skirt of the Gigantona and walks around with her. The large puppet is accompanied by a dwarf named Pepe who dances around her and recites ballads.

These figures were especially important during the war between the Sandinistas and Somoza. In campaigns to free political prisoners being held by the National Guard, Subtiavans would bring the Gigantona and Pepe. Pepe recited political verses that brought attention to the unfair treatment of prisoners. The Subtiavans and their Gigantona also visited the homes of Somoza's supporters. There, with the Gigantona dancing and Pepe reading poems, they accused those people of siding with Somoza.

People everywhere have a need to express themselves and find meaning in life. For Nicaraguans, expression may mean talking with a friend, painting a picture, or performing a play. Finding meaning in life may involve a belief in God and attending Catholic mass.

A Changing Religion

Along Nicaragua's Atlantic coast, most people belong to the Protestant church. There are many Moravian churches in this part of the country. The majority of Nicaraguans, though, are Roman Catholic.

For centuries the Catholic church tried to hold on to traditions and discourage change. Until recently, priests said mass in Latin even though the people attending mass understood only Spanish. The church was supposed to be a place where people forgot their daily worries here on earth. They were to think instead about God in heaven.

The Catholic church in Nicaragua and the rest of Latin America is undergoing a change. In 1968 a group of priests met at a conference in Medellín, Colombia, where they discussed an idea called liberation theology. Liberation theology is meant to free people from their lives of poverty. In order to do so, say the priests who preach liberation theology, people must be willing to take an active part in changing their lives. For the first time many people were told that it was not God's will for them to be poor. Many peasants began to believe that perhaps they were poor because landowners and other powerful Nicaraguans were so rich.

Some Nicaraguans don't believe in liberation theology. They don't believe that religion should be "political" and encourage people to try to change their lives. These people may not agree with Nicaraguans who say their religion brought them to support the Sandinistas. They think some people are born rich and others are born poor—and since that is the way God intended the world to be, the church should not try to change it.

Yet the churches and ministers who preach liberation theology are popular among more and more Nicaraguans. Many of these same people joined in the struggle to force Somoza to give up his absolute power. They know what can happen if people organize to make changes and don't believe that God wants anyone to be poor or poorly treated.

Nicaraguan life is changing rapidly. Since 1968 the religion of many people has changed because of liberation theology. Since 1979 the arts and attitudes about the arts, among many other things, have been affected by the Sandinista revolution.

Nicaraguans have been forced to respond to change—whether they want it or not. By writing poetry and painting murals, they can express how they feel about these changes. At the same time, Nicaraguans hope to hold on to and learn more about the culture of their ancestors. Through studying their cultural history, they hope to gain a better understanding of their modern culture.

3. A Long and Troubled Past

West of downtown Managua there is a tiny national park with footprints preserved in hardened lava. The footprints, both human and animal, are heading toward Lake Managua. Scientists assume that the people and animals were fleeing from an erupting volcano. They estimate the footprints to be two to five thousand years old. Nothing else is known about these ancient people.

An Indian Heritage

Little is known about early people who lived in Nicaragua because few ruins or objects made by them remain. As far as historians and scientists know, the first two Indian tribes in what is now Nicaragua were the Nahua and Caribs. The Caribs lived mainly in the south along Lake Nicaragua and the Pacific Ocean. The Niqui-ranos, descendants of the Nahuas, lived in the southwest corner of Nicaragua. Their chief was Nicarao. Nica-raocalli, which today is the city of Rivas, was their capital.

The Chorotegas, who came from Mexico, lived in the northwest corner of Nicaragua. In the central region were the Chontales, who some historians think were descendants of the Maya Indians. By this time the Caribs lived in the Atlantic coast region of the country. The Chontales and Caribs were mainly hunters and warriors. They lived in houses called *chozas*, made of tree branches.

The Chorotegas and Niquiranos in the west made pottery and weavings. They cultivated corn, yucca, and tobacco, and hunted deer and birds. Their houses were made of stones and mud.

Each Indian tribe had its own organization. The chief of the Niquiranos wore special clothing and was assisted by a council of elders. The Niquiranos believed in several gods, each of whom ruled over something in the natural world. There was a god of the sun and a god of corn. Since the Indians believed in another life, when they died their possessions were buried along with them. They thought they would need their possessions in the next life.

The Indians used cacao seeds for money and traded them when they needed other products. Their marketplace was called Tiangue. In order to get there, they had just two forms of transportation—canoeing and walking.

The tribes spoke many different languages. They also communicated by writing hieroglyphics on a special paper made from the bark of a tree. Hieroglyphics are symbols that make up messages or stories.

In 1502, on his fourth and final trip to the New World, Christopher Columbus sailed to Nicaragua and claimed the land for Spain. At that time there were three main Indian tribes in the region. The Sumo, hunters along the northern border, and the Miskito, fishermen along the Caribbean, were both nomadic, which means they traveled from place to place. On the western shore of Lake Nicaragua, the Nicarao Indians lived in villages and farmed the maize, cotton, and cacao in the surrounding fields.

The Rule of the Spaniards

When the Spaniards arrived, they surprised and frightened the Indians. The Spaniards brought strange animals with them—horses which the Indians had never seen before. The Spaniards also brought guns. Because the Indians had no firearms, they were unable to stop the strangers from invading their land.

Several things changed for the Indians after the Spaniards settled in Nicaragua. Since the Spaniards didn't understand the Indian language, they began to use the wrong names for various places. They changed Itztetli to Estelí and Xiloatil to Jiloa. Nahuolotli became Nagarote, and Masaltyan became Masaya.

The Spanish conquest also changed the way of life in Nicaragua. Many of the Indian traditions were lost, while other traditions were blended with Spanish traditions when the Spaniards and Indians intermarried. The new seeds, plants, and animals from Spain created different forms of agriculture. Tobacco farming became a business. Cattle raising was introduced. Cloth, oils, and sugar were produced and traded with Spain and the rest of Central America. Foods and clothing changed. The Spaniards also brought the Catholic religion, and Catholic missionaries started schools. A Spanish governor lived in León and ruled the country. Before long the Spanish way of life had spread throughout Nicaragua.

Thousands of Indians died because the Spaniards introduced new diseases to which the Indians had no resistance. The Spaniards forced the Indians to work the land they had taken from them and made themselves masters over the Indians.

Sometimes the Spaniards tried to fool the Indians in order to change their ways. In Subtiava, on the edge of present-day León, the Spaniards painted a bright yellow sun with a smiling face on the ceiling of the cathedral. Since the Spaniards knew that the Indians worshiped the sun, they thought the painting would bring people to mass. Once the Indians were there, the Spaniards hoped to convert them to Christianity. The cathedral in Subtiava is one of the oldest churches in the Western Hemisphere. The bright yellow sun still smiles down on the people who worship there today.

The Spaniards brought the Catholic religion to Nicaragua and built large cathedrals such as this one in León.

In 1570 Nicaragua became part of the Captaincy General of Guatemala after fighting off attempts by the English pirates Drake and Hawkins to take over the country. For many years all of Central America was ruled by Spain, despite several attempts to gain independence. On September 15, 1821, Nicaragua and the other Central American countries declared their independence from Spain. They later joined the Mexican empire, but left it a year later. In 1823 they formed the United Provinces of Central America.

Americans in Nicaragua

Because of disagreements with the other countries, Nicaragua left the union in 1838 and founded its own republic. By this time two main political groups, the conservatives of Granada and the liberals of León, had begun competing for power. In 1855 William Walker, a private citizen of the United States, set out with his small army of California fighting men to help the liberals gain power. Unknown to them, Walker planned to save the Nicaraguans from what he believed was an inability to govern themselves.

When he arrived in Nicaragua, he assembled an army of Indian volunteers to fight with his own men. By the following year Walker had defeated the conservatives of Nicaragua as well as the combined armies of all the other countries of Central America. Before long land that had been owned by Nicaraguans was in the hands of U.S. companies. When the liberals who had been his supporters started to object, Walker took complete control of the government and made himself president of Nicaragua in 1856. As president he declared English the official language and made slavery legal. A year after he arrived, the liberals and conservatives joined forces and drove Walker out of the country.

The U.S. government first became involved in Nicaraguan affairs because of that nation's location in the

world. For many years the United States wanted to
build a canal across Nicaragua to link the Atlantic and
Pacific oceans. In 1901, Nicaraguan President Zelaya
set limits on U.S. rights to the canal because he didn't
want the United States to control Nicaragua. The
United States decided to build the canal in Panama
instead of accepting the Nicaraguan terms.

In 1909 a revolt broke out against Zelaya, who was
a harsh ruler. The United States sided with the rebels,
and Zelaya was driven out of office. The United States
began to lend money to Nicaragua under the condition
that Nicaragua would allow U.S. businesses to operate
there. When Nicaraguan forces organized to oppose
U.S. control, the U.S. marines were sent to Nicaragua in
1912. For twenty-one years, until 1933, the marines
remained in Nicaragua in order to supervise elections
and protect U.S. interests.

A Revolutionary Hero

During the 1930s a man named Augusto César
Sandino organized a rebel force to remove the marines
from Nicaragua. He has been an important figure in
Nicaraguan history ever since that time. Sandino was
born in 1895 in an Indian village in southern Nicaragua.
His father owned and managed coffee plantations, and
his mother was a peasant of Indian ancestry. Sandino

Augusto César Sandino was a revolutionary leader who has become an important figure in Nicaraguan history.

attended primary school as a boy. Later he studied bookkeeping because his father wanted him to run the family coffee plantations and other farms.

Sandino left home and worked on a sugar plantation in Honduras and for the United Fruit Company in Guatemala from 1921 to 1925. Then he went to Mexico and worked for an oil company. At this time the unions organized to protect workers' rights and began struggling against the U.S. companies that owned Mexico's oil. Sandino believed the workers were being treated poorly. He felt he understood their cause.

When he returned to Nicaragua, Sandino searched for people to fight for an independent Nicaragua. "Only bullets will make Nicaragua free," Sandino said. "It's better to die a rebel than live as a slave." The first to join him in his fight against the U.S. Marines were twenty-nine miners in San Albino. They came to call themselves "Sandinistas" after their leader. Before going to war, Sandino married Blanca Arauz, a telegraph operator who became active in her husband's struggle.

The war took its toll on the Sandinistas, but Sandino refused all offers to surrender. "We are not soldiers. We are the people. We are armed civilians," he said. By now he had a force of six thousand, many of whom were women. The Sandinistas captured the town of Ocotal but were eventually defeated by U.S. military air power. Sandino and his forces were defeated several more times before he decided to try guerrilla warfare. In guerrilla warfare small bands of soldiers surprise their enemies by ambushing them and forcing them to change their plans. Although he realized he could not win against the U.S. forces, Sandino and his army continued to fight. "Free homeland or death," Sandino declared.

A Family of Dictators

In 1933 the U.S. Marines left Nicaragua, leaving a new Nicaraguan army, the National Guard, in their place. President Sacasa, then president of Nicaragua, and Sandino signed a peace treaty ending the fighting and promising land for the Sandinistas. The man the United States made commander of the Nicaraguan National Guard was named Anastasio Somoza García. This was the beginning of more than forty years of Somoza family rule.

Anastasio Somoza was born in 1896 in San Marcos, a town near Sandino's birthplace. Somoza was from a wealthy coffee-growing family. As a young man he married Salvadora Debayle Sacasa, the niece of President Sacasa. Before he joined the army, Somoza worked as a used car dealer and a health inspector. He had traveled to the United States, where he had learned English and studied at Pierce Commercial College in Philadelphia.

When he was named commander of the National Guard, Somoza immediately concentrated on gaining power and wealth. His political ambition knew few limits, and he used the power he had to make himself wealthy. In 1934, after the marines had left Nicaragua, Somoza had members of the National Guard kill Sandino. In the days following the murder, the guard killed more than three hundred Sandinistas. President Sacasa was angered by the violence and tried to control the guard, but Somoza acted first. In 1936 he forced Sacasa to resign and made himself president a year later.

Anastasio Somoza, sometimes called "Tacho," treated Nicaragua as if it were his personal property. In twenty years he became owner of cattle ranches, land, banks, shops, baseball teams, and industries. He was disliked by the majority of the Nicaraguan people. At a ball in his honor in León in 1956, Somoza was assassinated by a student and poet named Rigoberto López Pérez.

The rule of the Somozas was not so easily ended. Somoza had already arranged for his sons, Luis and Anastasio, to assume positions of power when he died. Luis was to be president. The younger son, Anastasio, or "Tachito," was to be head of the National Guard.

Luis Somoza freed political prisoners and allowed some freedom of the press when he became president. He also announced that presidents could not be reelected or pass the position on to their children. Anastasio "Tachito" Somoza was elected president for the 1967 to 1971 term. Many Nicaraguans believed that the elections were not free and honest, however.

As both president and head of the National Guard, the youngest Somoza had complete power over Nicaragua. He used that power to continue to increase the family wealth. Within a few years he owned one-fifth of the land in Nicaragua, three of the country's six sugar mills, 168 factories, an airline, a radio and television station, and banks. The workers on his farms were soldiers paid by funds from the national budget. The Somoza family's wealth was estimated at nine hundred million dollars, yet Nicaragua was one of the poorest countries on earth. Across Nicaragua the people were unemployed, poorly fed, and unable to read and write. Many children died because they didn't have the food they needed.

As the daily lives of the people became more and more difficult, some Nicaraguans came to believe that major change was necessary to improve their lives. Since elections in Nicaragua, these people believed, were not free and honest, they had to use other means to make changes. In the towns across Nicaragua, small groups of guerrillas began to form. They wanted to remove Somoza from office and give land and political power to the Nicaraguan people.

Members of the Sandinista army fought against the rule of Anastasio Somoza Debayle during the 1970s.

The People Unite and Win

The FSLN, which stands for "Sandinista National Liberation Front," was formed in 1961. In its early years it was made up mostly of students and workers. They educated themselves and others about the history of their country and about the FSLN's beliefs and goals. The FSLN said its main goal was to help the poor by teaching them to read and write, providing health care, food, and housing, and giving political power to the workers and peasants.

It was dangerous to be a member of the FSLN or

to know someone who was. The National Guard imprisoned and killed many members of the FSLN, or Sandinistas as they were sometimes called. In 1967, during a demonstration against Tachito Somoza's election, the guard opened fire on the crowd. The attack left nearly 400 people dead in the center of Managua. Because it was dangerous to oppose the Somoza government, many Nicaraguans did not join the guerrillas even though they agreed with the Sandinistas.

During the 1970s, two events created strong opposition to Somoza and increased support for the FSLN. The first was the 1972 earthquake in Managua, which killed 5,000 people and left 3,000 homeless. Countries around the world sent money, food, clothing, and medicine to survivors of the earthquake. The FSLN charged that many of the supplies never reached them because Somoza and the National Guard kept a large amount of the money and goods for themselves.

More people turned to the FSLN in 1978 when Pedro Joaquín Chamorro, director of the newspaper *La Prensa* ("The Press"), was murdered. Chamorro was loved by most Nicaraguans because he dared to stand up to Somoza and print articles about Somoza's abuse of power. Many people believed that Somoza had arranged for Chamorro to be killed. Fifty thousand demonstrators attended his funeral procession. Thousands more were turned away. During a mass workers' strike that followed the funeral, there were huge demonstrations and bloody clashes with the National Guard. *Las Doce* ("The Twelve"), a group of twelve men from the Catholic church, business, and university, demanded that Somoza step down.

By this time the conflict between the FSLN and the National Guard had developed into a full-scale war. The Sandinistas began to win many victories. They had the support of most Nicaraguans. When Somoza could see that the FSLN would win the war, he fled to Miami, just two days before the Sandinista victory on July 19, 1979. A year later, while Somoza was living in Paraguay, South America, he was killed by a bomb that destroyed his car.

The Sandinista victory came with much human loss. Forty thousand people were dead; 200,000 families were homeless; 40,000 children were orphans; 750,000 people were without food; 1 million people were refugees. The new Sandinista government, called the Junta of National Reconstruction, was faced with trying to provide the basic needs of the people.

The junta was a small group of leaders that ruled the country for five years before Nicaraguans were allowed to vote for their government. At first leaders from a number of political groups that had joined forces against Somoza served in the junta. Then the leaders who did not agree with the Sandinista's new policies left the government. Gilbert Coe, a leader of the Social Democratic party, is one of those who has spoken out strongly against the Sandinista government. On the occasion of the seventh anniversary of the 1979 revolution, he said: "It means that for seven years, the dreams of the Nicaraguan people for social justice, democracy, and freedom of speech have been frustrated."

Women played an important role in the Sandinista victory. By the final battles in 1979, three out of ten members of the Sandinista army were women. Dora Maria Tellez, Monica Baltodano, and Leticia Herrera were commanders in the army. Dora Maria Tellez and Daisy Zamora took part in a Sandinista attack on the National Palace. Nora Astorga was a political leader of four guerrilla units. Many other women played major roles in other guerrilla operations.

The women's organization, AMNLAE, is named for Luisa Espinosa, the first woman of the FSLN to die during the struggle. AMNLAE works to improve conditions for women as workers, mothers, and wives. A month after taking office, the Sandinista government passed a law providing equal rights for women.

The Nation's New Leader

Today the Nicaraguan government is made up of the National Assembly and a three-member coordinating committee. Several political parties are represented in the National Assembly, which meets regularly to vote on proposed laws. Daniel Ortega was elected president of the country in 1984 in an election his opponents claimed was unfair. Before he was elected president, Ortega had served as coordinator of the Sandinista government.

Ortega spent many years fighting Somoza before the Sandinista victory in 1979. He was born in 1945 in Libertad in the department of Chontales, a mining area in the central region of the country. Ortega's grandfather had fought with Sandino in the 1930s. Ortega's mother was a cashier in the mines, and his father worked as an accountant. Both his mother and father were imprisoned during the rule of the first Somoza.

Soon after Ortega's birth the family moved to Juigalpa, and later to Managua. Ortega was a quiet, serious child who was active in the Catholic church and from an early age gave Bible lessons in the poor areas of Managua. As a student he attended demonstrations against Somoza. He was first arrested for demonstrating when he was sixteen.

By the time he entered the Central American University in Managua, Ortega was a member of the FSLN. He was arrested for his involvement in the FSLN and spent seven years in jail. In the first days after his arrest, he was severely tortured. While Ortega was in

Daniel Ortega (in uniform) *and another Sandinista government official.*

prison, he and his companions scheduled their days full of activities. In the morning they did running exercises. Later in the day they studied. Ortega read stacks of books about law, history, and geography. He also wrote poetry, which he sent to family members and friends.

Ortega and other Sandinista leaders have received training in the Soviet Union and believe in the ideas of Karl Marx. Since Communist countries attempt to follow Marx's teachings, Ortega has been called a Communist by the U.S. government and some Nicaraguan leaders. According to Marx, wealth should be earned and shared by everyone. Marx believed that certain human freedoms should be limited so that a society without classes—of rich and poor—would be created.

Although Ortega is a hero to many, not all Nicaraguans like him. People who support the contras, and some who don't agree with either side, want the Sandinistas removed from the government. Since 1980, a year after the Sandinistas came to power, Nicaraguan territory has been attacked by thousands of contra fighters. The contras are opposed to the revolution and to the changes the Sandinistas are making.

The Contra War

The contra war is largely a war against agriculture, on which the country depends for its food supply and for earning money from exports. The contras kill livestock, burn warehouses filled with agricultural goods, attack roads on which crops are taken to market, and kill the people who work in the fields. The contras have also killed Nicaraguans who are not involved in farming. In a 1985 raid, they killed nine mothers traveling in army trucks to visit their sons serving in the army.

In 1984, Americas Watch, a respected international human rights organization, reported that the largest contra group, the FDN, "has engaged repeatedly in torture and murder of unarmed citizens." The contra organizations deny that their forces attack farm and health workers and say their battle is only with the Sandinista government. But since the contras have been fighting to overthrow the Sandinista government, hundreds of civilians have been killed by the rebels.

The FDN operates out of bases along the Honduran-Nicaraguan border in the north. Forty-six of the forty-eight FDN military commanders are former members of Somoza's National Guard. The contras who operated along the Costa Rican border until 1986 refused to unite with the FDN because of its link with the National Guard. Eden Pastora, the former commander of the southern group, surrendered to Costa Rican officials in May 1986. "We think there is no possibility of a military victory," said Pastora, a former FSLN member who disagreed with the policies of the Sandinistas.

The contras attacked and destroyed this bus near Estelí in northern Nicaragua.

Contras along the Atlantic coast are somewhat different from those in western Nicaragua. Many of their goals are the same, but these contras have different reasons for disliking the Sandinista government.

A Proud and Independent People

Since the eastern and western parts of the country are so separate from one another, there is sometimes little understanding between them. In the late 1600s the British were the main power along the eastern coast. The British taught the Miskitos a hatred of the Spaniards. The Miskitos have a word that means both "Spaniard" and "our enemy." Likewise, Nicaraguans from the west coast sometimes look down on people from the Atlantic coast, calling them *los hermanitos de la costa* ("the little brothers of the coast").

Sandino was not a hero on the Atlantic coast because he was a mestizo from the west. The revolution in 1979 was fought in western Nicaragua. People on the Atlantic coast were far removed from the fighting.

During the rule of the Somozas, the Atlantic coast inhabitants were neglected. Yet they liked the fact that no one from the west interfered with their lives. When the Sandinistas came to power, they wanted to bring the east and west together. They made some mistakes in the process, partly because they didn't understand the cultural differences of the Atlantic coast people. Because of such problems and because they were suspicious of Miskitos involved with the contras, the Sandinista soldiers killed some Miskito Indians in 1981 and 1982. Many of the Indians were arrested and imprisoned.

The government has also forced thousands of Miskito, Sumo, and Rama Indians to move away from the Rio Coco and other areas of contra fighting. The Indians resented being moved away from their homes and were even more angry when government soldiers burned many of their villages. The Sandinistas say they moved people away from areas of contra danger. The Indians believe they were forced to move because the government was afraid they were contra supporters. They say that when a hungry man with a gun shows up at your door asking for food, you give it to him. It doesn't matter if he's a contra or a Sandinista.

The Indians claim they have been caught in the middle of the war between the Sandinista and contra armies. The government has admitted that it made mistakes in dealing with the Miskitos. Thousands of Miskitos have now returned to their homes. According to a 1984 Americas Watch report, "the government has made substantial progress with the release of those held in prison, and the more careful procedures for investigation and arrests in the Atlantic coast area."

The contras in the Atlantic coast region also forced many people to move, usually to contra camps or refugee camps in Honduras. Many were then made soldiers in the contra army, often against their wishes.

Thousands of people on the Atlantic coast, perhaps as many as half of them, want to separate from western Nicaragua and form their own country with its own government. Because the relationship between the east and west has become so tense, in some areas the Sandinista soldiers have agreed to point their guns at the

These children live in Puerto Cabezas on Nicaragua's Atlantic coast.

ground and look straight ahead when passing through town. However, not all people on the Atlantic coast support the contras. Some support the Sandinistas and believe the government wants to help them.

CIA Troops or "Freedom Fighters"?

The contras receive funds from the U.S. government. Some of the money is sent directly to the contras;

other funds have been channeled through the Central Intelligence Agency (CIA). The CIA has plotted secretly to overthrow the Sandinista government. In 1983, for example, the CIA worked with the contras to bomb the Managua airport and blow up major oil pipelines at several ports. The CIA directed the operation that placed explosive mines in the harbor at the port of Corinto. The U.S. secret agency hoped the mines would blow up ships entering the harbor.

Nicaragua protested the mining of the harbor of Corinto and other U.S. actions in support of the contras. It took its case to the International Court of Justice, or World Court, the judicial arm of the United Nations. In June 1986 the World Court ruled that the U.S. government was at fault for "training, arming, equipping, financing, and supplying the contra forces." The court also found that the United States had no right to mine Nicaraguan harbors and stage armed attacks on these harbors and nearby oil storage tanks. Before the judgment of the court was announced, the U.S. government had said it would ignore any ruling by the international judges. The World Court has no power to enforce its decisions.

One Nicaraguan who provided written testimony for the World Court was Edgar Chamorro. Chamorro, a wealthy Nicaraguan who lives in Miami, is a former director of the FDN. He no longer works for the contras because he disapproves of their actions.

In addition to the CIA, other U.S. government agencies may have attempted to provide secret aid to the contra forces. In November 1986, President Reagan announced that the United States had secretly sold weapons to Iran. Later that month, the president revealed that members of his National Security Council staff had sent money from the arms sales to contra forces. Sending this money may have been against the law, because at the time it was sent, the U.S. Congress had prohibited any government funding of these forces. Congress and special commissions began investigations immediately. The long-term effects of the secret funding on U.S. policy toward Central America are uncertain.

Several members of the U.S. Congress and human rights groups have charged the FDN and its financial supporters with illegal activity. They accuse these groups of shipping arms from New Orleans to Managua, selling cocaine to raise money, and breaking a U.S. law—the Neutrality Act. The Neutrality Act says the United States cannot carry out or direct military attacks against a country with which the United States is not at war. All three charges are being investigated.

The Reagan administration chooses to support the contras because it does not agree with the Sandinista government and its goals. President Reagan calls the contras "freedom fighters" and says "The Sandinista rule is a Communist reign of terror." He also claims the current Nicaraguan government denies its people certain rights and freedoms. "The Sandinista revolution in Nicaragua turned out to be just an exchange of one set of autocratic [unjust] rulers for another, and the people still have no freedom, no democratic rights, and more poverty," President Reagan says.

From the point of view of the U.S. government, the Sandinistas don't believe in freedom and democracy and want to spread Communism throughout Central America. According to President Reagan, Nicaragua is in danger of becoming a base for Soviet-backed military attacks against other nations. Once the Communists, working through the Sandinistas, have taken over Nicaragua, Reagan believes, they will send arms to guerrillas fighting against other Central American governments. If the United States does not aid the contras in their fight against the Sandinistas, says Reagan, all of Central America may fall before Communist-supported revolutions. And if the Central American nations fall, says the president, then Mexico and other nearby countries may suffer the same fate.

Questions about the Future

The Sandinistas respond by saying that theirs is a young government still in the process of reaching its goals. They want to be allowed to choose their own future, even when that means making mistakes. "We had good relations and good communications with [former President] Carter's administration," says President Ortega. "The problem is that President Reagan has always had a closed position on Latin America."

The Sandinistas point out that although their government accepts money and military aid from Cuba, it is not a Communist dictatorship and does not use Cuba as a model. The Sandinista government turned to Cuba, the Soviet Union, and countries in Eastern Europe for aid in order to fight the U.S.-backed contras. Nicaraguan troops are trained by Cuban and Soviet military advisers, say the Sandinistas, because they welcome assistance from any countries that offer it. The Sandinistas say they want to be on good terms with as many countries as possible. The Nicaraguan government also claims that if it weren't at war with the United States, it would depend far less on the Soviet Union and Cuba and be a more democratic country than it is today.

The Sandinistas believe their form of government is something new, not something borrowed from another country. Nearly two out of three farms are privately owned, while the rest are government farms and cooperatives. In a true Communist country, people do not own farms and factories.

In response to President Reagan's statements about

Like these young people, many Nicaraguans now live in agricultural cooperatives. Two out of three farms, though, are privately owned.

lack of freedom in Nicaragua, the Sandinistas point out that their country has several political parties. However, *La Prensa*, the newspaper critical of the government, was closed because the Sandinistas believe the paper supports the contras and discourages young men from being drafted into the Nicaraguan army. The government declared a state of emergency in October 1985 to acquire the powers it claims are needed in a time of war. It used these emergency powers to close *La Prensa.*

It has also used these powers to arrest political and labor union leaders who have criticized the government. A number of opposition leaders have been arrested, held for questioning, and put on trial before "popular tribunals." According to Amnesty International, a well-known human rights group, some of the leaders have been sentenced to jail unfairly based on false government evidence.

The Sandinistas claim that there is freedom of religion in Nicaragua. In fact, three Catholic priests head the government departments of foreign relations, culture, and the national youth movement. Yet Cardinal Obando y Bravo disagrees with the Nicaraguan government about the extent of religious freedom.

Cardinal Obando y Bravo was an outspoken critic of the Somoza government, and he won the respect of the FSLN in the 1970s. Since 1980, however, he has not supported the Sandinistas. Obando believes that the government doesn't allow freedom of expression for all priests and pastors. He warns people about the dangers of Communism in his sermons. In 1983 Obando and eight bishops wrote a pastoral letter urging young Nicaraguan men to resist the military draft.

In the summer of 1985 the government forced ten foreign priests to leave Nicaragua for delivering antigovernment sermons. It also shut down the Catholic radio station and refused to allow a Catholic bishop to return to the country from a foreign trip. The government claims it is not opposed to religion in general. Instead, it says, it is opposed to religious leaders who preach antigovernment sermons and tell young men not to be drafted into the military.

In addition to these church leaders, several political parties do not agree with the Sandinista government. Opposition parties hold rallies, post billboards, and publish newsletters. In 1984, claim the parties, they were not given enough freedom to campaign to have any real chance of winning the election. The Reagan administration also charged that the election was controlled by the Sandinistas, but a number of international observers disagree with that claim. These election watchers say the election was among the fairest in Central American history. The Canadian Church and Human Rights Delegation and Irish Inter-Parliamentary Delegation both claim the election was free and fair. Nearly two-thirds of the voters supported the FSLN, the party of Daniel Ortega and the Sandinistas.

Several Latin American nations are working for peace in Central America. Mexico, Panama, Colombia, and Venezuela make up the Contadora group, formed in 1983. The Contadora countries call for a political rather than a military solution to the conflicts in Central

America. These concerned nations have drafted an agreement that could limit the size of Central American armies. President Ortega claims such limits are unfair as long as his country is at war. "The United States wants to use the Contadora negotiations [talks] to make Nicaragua disarm and fall," he says.

Signs of Hope

In Nicaragua, as in countries everywhere, the government tries to make things look better than they are. Yet there have been some major improvements in the daily lives of most of the people. Under Somoza, Nicaragua had the lowest life expectancy at birth—the number of years a person is expected to live—in Central America. It also had one of the highest levels of infant death—the number of young children who die—in the region. In a 1986 report, UNICEF, a United Nations group, found that Nicaragua's infant death rate fell by 30 percent in four years starting in 1979. This is one of the best records ever achieved by a developing nation.

One of the reasons many young children are no longer dying is proper medical care. Not a single case of polio has been reported in Nicaragua since 1981. Nicaragua was declared a "model country in medical attention" by the Organization of American States in 1983. The World Health Organization has singled out Nica-

In Nicaragua today, children like this young girl have a better chance than ever before to grow up and become adults because they receive proper medical care.

ragua's health program as one of five model approaches to health care in developing countries.

Since 1979 more than a million Nicaraguans have been involved in some kind of formal schooling. Thousands learned to read and write during a national literacy campaign. More than 1,200 new schools have been built, most of them in the countryside.

More than 40,000 landless Nicaraguans now have the use of land where they can grow food. Production of basic foods such as corn, beans, and rice has increased at least 50 percent since 1979. Since these are the foods most Nicaraguans eat daily, their diet has improved greatly. The current government wants Nicaragua to be able to feed its own people.

Today, however, basic foods are in short supply. One reason for the lack of food is the strict government controls on the prices farmers charge for their crops. Also, the government does not have the money it needs to help the country's farmers produce more food. Nicaragua's agriculture minister said "our problem is. . .that we cannot use our money for normal purposes, for development, because we have to support a war."

The Struggle Continues

As the contra war continues, it becomes more difficult for the government to continue improving the so-

Children practice how to protect themselves in a bomb shelter. The Nicaraguan government spends more than half of its budget on the armed forces because of the contra war.

cial welfare programs it has introduced. At the markets throughout the country there are shortages of some items—one week, not enough toilet paper; another week, too little sugar—in part due to the contra war. Supporting the armed forces requires more than 50 percent of the national budget. The Sandinistas, former guerrillas themselves, know all too well how difficult it is to defend themselves in a guerrilla war like the one the contras are fighting.

Nicaraguans are tired of war. Forty thousand people died in the revolution against Somoza, and more than 30,000 soldiers, farm workers, and others on both sides have died in the contra war since 1980. Nicaraguan leaders fear that U.S. military forces will invade their country. "If peace does not come and war continues, and with it the possibility of a North American military intervention [attack], the whole world should know that the people—barefoot, in rags, and hungry—will fight to the end," says President Ortega.

The people of Nicaragua wait for the war to end. They hope and pray that it will end soon. Their country has been at war for many years. Although they don't like war and can't get used to it, they know that they must go about their daily work as they have always done. Often politics is not the part of life many Nicaraguan people consider most important. What matters is having enough food to eat, a home to live in, family, friends, and a peaceful community.

4. *Stories from East and West*

Nicaraguans have hundreds of stories and legends. Most of them have been passed down from one generation to the next without ever having been written down. Now there are some books that contain collections of these stories. There are several versions of all of the stories, depending on the part of the country they are from and depending on who is telling the story. These first two stories are from the Miskito Indians who live on the Atlantic Coast. *Sukling kwakwalhra* is the Miskito name for "The Proud Toad."

The Proud Toad

The buzzards were going to have a big party up in the clouds, and they invited all the birds. The young toad heard about the invitation, and he wanted to go, too. Then he thought, "But how am I going to go? I don't know how to fly."

The hawk flew by and told the toad that he was going to the buzzards' party. "They invited me, too," said the toad, "but I am going to arrive later. There is something I wanted to ask you. In this bag I have my bamboo flute. Would you be able to carry it? I am going to play the flute to make the party festive. When we meet up at the buzzards' party, you can deliver the flute to me."

The hawk agreed to carry the flute. And then, in a wink—without being noticed by the hawk—the toad jumped into the bag. The hawk began flying. He flew and flew and finally arrived at the party in the clouds. The hawk left the bag on a corner of the house and went over to flirt with a female hawk.

Without being seen by any birds, the toad very slowly crept out of the bag. He took his flute and began to play: "Ruku, ruku, ruku." He played all night without sleeping.

At dawn the hawk ran into the road and asked him, "And you, how are you going to get down from here without wings?" The toad laughed and proudly said, "Everyone arrived here flying, and I arrived here flying, too."

When the party ended, the birds said good-bye to the buzzards and flew down to earth, each returning to his or her own house. The only one that didn't have wings, of course, was our friend the toad. He was very worried about how he was going to get down out of the clouds. He grabbed his flute and jumped into the sack, thinking that perhaps the hawk would remember the sack and come back to get it. But the hawk forgot the poor toad up in the clouds.

The buzzards cleaned their houses before going down to earth. In their hurry they grabbed and threw the bag that was on the corner of the house. Since the toad was inside the bag, he fell from the clouds very quickly. "Ooh, ooh, ooh," he screamed, opening his legs and pretending he was flying. When he came down like this, the hawk looked at him and asked, "Toad friend, are you having problems?"

"No," said the toad. "Didn't you know I was coming down?" he asked, opening his legs as if they were wings. He fell against a rock and splat—he fell flat on his belly.

Since that time, all toads are flat. And when the sky is cloudy, the toads always sing, "Ruku, ruku, ruku, pic, pic, pic" for the sun to come out again. Our toads say that if the sun comes out again, the buzzards in their house in the clouds will have another party.

The second Miskito story, *Mani wihki li piua wal kisika*, means "The Story of Summer and Winter." Along the Atlantic coast of Nicaragua, as everywhere, the seasons bring good and bad things. For instance, rain helps crops grow, but too much rain causes floods that damage or kill them. Stories like this one are started because people need to try to understand and explain the weather. The weather is something that we have no control over. We can try to understand it, but we can't change it.

A Miskito mother and child.

The Story of Summer and Winter

One day Summer said to Winter, "How bad you are! You kill the people when you make floods. The seas, rivers, and lagoons overflow with water. No one likes you for this reason. But look, everyone likes me."

Winter answered, "You are worse. Because when you work you kill animals, trees—and even kill people."

Since they couldn't agree, Winter made a suggestion. "Come on, Summer, we will divide the year into two parts. You will get one part, and I will get the other. I am going to show you that I work better than you."

Summer accepted the suggestion. First Summer worked and worked without rest for six months. The plants dried up, and many children and animals died from the heat.

Then Winter said to Summer, "Your work has not been good because you have killed plants, animals, and children. Now it is my turn."

Winter began to work. He worked and rested, worked and rested. When he rested, the sun came out and the water dried up. When Winter worked again, it rained. The plants and animals became healthy again, and the children didn't die of heat now.

With the rain the plants grew, the animals fattened up, and the children were happy. With the sun the fruits ripened, and everyone had enough food.

"Yes," Summer answered Winter. "You are right. Because I didn't rest and worked too much, I hurt the children, animals, and plants. Now let's work in another way. I am going to work, and then I am going to rest so that you can work."

The two agreed to work it out this way. Since that time, Summer works and rests a while. Winter also works a while and waters the land. And that is why there is a spell of rain during the summer. In the same way, Winter works a little and then rests while Summer works to give warmth to the children, plants, and animals.

Stories and legends from the west coast have less to do with animals and nature and more to do with ghosts, devils, and evil spirits. There are ghost stories about the *segua*, an enchanted woman who goes out at night and lets out a whistling sound. And there are stories about people who have a pact, or an agreement, with the devil in order to get rich.

Once a person has made this pact, he or she becomes possessed by the devil, the stories go. The person who is possessed by the devil has the ability to change humans to animals, or to treat humans like animals. Some Nicaraguans believe that only a person who sells his or her soul to the devil can be a cruel master and treat workers like animals.

El Punche de Oro de los subtiavas ("The Gold Crab

A Nicaraguan father reads a book to his son.

of the Subtiavas") is a story from the Indian community of Subtiava. It is about the magic of a community and the pride of the Indian people.

The Gold Crab of the Subtiavas

There is a courageous ghost which comes out at night. When he comes out of the raging waves of the Pacific, he is surrounded by a blinding light. He drags himself out of the water and on to the community of Subtiava. This ghost, this great ball of fire, stops in front of the main door of the church of Subtiava. He stops to worship the sun, which is painted on the ceiling of the church.

People who live in Subtiava say there is a huge buried treasure in their community. "The spirit of this treasure comes out at night," they say. "The spirit is the huge Gold Crab. People who have seen it say it is a huge crab that shines like gold. All who have tried to grab it are unable to do so. Those who try fall just before they reach it and are left without speech for several days. The crab is the spirit of the treasure in an Indian community. It started coming out at night after the last Indian leader died at the hands of the Spaniards."

Some people claim they have seen the Gold Crab. Word reached Subtiava that one time his blinding light was seen at a hill near the town of San Isidro. That hill has been a strange place ever since, say some people who live near it. They say that no matter how often the deer there are shot, they are never killed. The trees are always heavy with fruit. The beautiful flowers never wither.

In the nearby town of León, everyone has heard about the Gold Crab. There are many witnesses who claim they have seen him. A man named Juan saw a blinding glare when he arrived at the Veracruz church one night. In the middle of his fright Juan decided to catch the Gold Crab. So he went running after the crab.

He caught up to the animal, but when he was going to grab it, it turned into a huge man the size of a giant.

As soon as the crab turned into a giant, Juan could no longer walk. His feet became heavy as if stones were tied around them. Finally he could not even move them. It was as if they were stuck in the earth. Juan spent a day or two with a fever, unable to walk or talk. He didn't speak until seven days later, after he got help from people who know how to cure these kinds of magic.

The crab still comes out twice a year. He comes out in the middle of Holy Week or shortly before, and in August. The Gold Crab comes out so that someday someone from Subtiava will catch him and gain his powers.

Many Nicaraguans believe that the Gold Crab in this legend is a buried treasure in the Indian community. The Gold Crab, they say, is like the spirit of the Indian people, which cannot be caught or taken away from them.

5. Nicaraguan Celebrations

Nicaraguans celebrate holidays and festivals year-round. Sometimes they get along without everyday needs in order to make holidays more enjoyable. After a hard day of work, Nicaraguans welcome the chance to dance, cook special foods, and spend time with friends and relatives. Many of the holidays are religious ones that have special meaning to Catholics.

Purísima

For Catholics in Nicaragua, *Purísima* ("The Virgin Mary") is one of the biggest and most important of all holidays. The holiday has its origin in *Volcán Cerro Negro* ("Black Hill Volcano"), which is located near León. In a time long ago that is lost in legend, the volcano erupted and caused the people much worry and trouble. Finally they set a statue of the Virgin Mary on the volcano, and it quit erupting. The people considered this event a miracle. Ever since they have had a celebration of the Virgin Mary called Purísima.

The preparations begin several weeks before the December 7 holiday. People make candy and paper baskets and buy lights and candles for the altar they

An altar to the Virgin Mary rests in a home during the celebration known as Purísima.

are going to build. The celebration begins the evening of December 6. Families in a few houses on every block in town build an altar to the Virgin Mary. They place a statue of Mary in front of their house and surround the statue with candles, lights, leaves, and flowers.

Guests start arriving at the altar in the evening. Folding chairs are set up for the guests so they can stop to pray at the altar. Before leaving, the host family gives each guest a piece of sugar cane, an orange, and a cold drink. Families who haven't built an altar go from house to house to pray and admire the altars. Those who are guests one year will be hosts the next. People take turns being hosts since it is expensive to build altars and entertain guests every year.

On December 7 people all over town set off fire-crackers and fireworks at sundown. Colorful displays fill the sky, but all of the noise is hard on the ears. Because of the huge crowds, the fireworks can also get very dangerous.

Later in the evening of December 7, children go from house to house with their parents to get treats. This evening is called *la gritería*, which means "the shouting." When people arrive at a house, they shout, "What brings us so much happiness?" The host shouts back, "The immaculate conception of Mary." Then the hosts hand out handmade baskets of colored paper filled with homemade candy. The people giving out the treats usually wear some sort of mask.

A Nicaraguan Christmas and Easter

In León, Purísima is an occasion for a bigger cele-bration than Christmas. In other parts of Nicaragua, Christmas, or *Navidad* in Spanish, is a more important holiday. Some houses have a Christmas tree decorated with lights and ornaments, or a large bare branch covered with cotton. On Christmas Eve those who can afford it have a special dinner of chicken or turkey and give toys to the children. At midnight on Christmas Eve, everyone in the city goes out onto the street and gives *abrazos de paz* ("hugs of peace") to their families and friends.

Most Catholic children receive a Christmas gift from their godparents at Christmastime. Being a godparent is an honor in Nicaragua. Godparents are responsible not only to see that the child is brought up in the religion, but also to look after the child's well being. In poor families, parents may not be able to give Christmas gifts to their own children. They often feel they must give gifts to their godchildren instead.

In Nicaragua, as in many other Catholic countries, *Pascua* ("Easter") and *Semana Santa* ("Holy Week") are important celebrations in Nicaragua. Catholics attend church much more during Lent and Easter than they do during the rest of the year. During Holy Week people march in processions that tell of Jesus' crucifixion, or death on the cross. In remembrance of Jesus' suffering, Good Friday is a sad and quiet day. Some women don't cook or allow their children to play, and peasants may not milk their cows. Holy Week is also a popular time for Nicaraguans to go to the beach. Baseball fans look forward to watching the Nicaraguan baseball play-offs, which are held during the week.

On September 24, the city of León celebrates its saint La Merced *with a procession through the streets.*

Saints and Family Holidays

Each town and village in western Nicaragua has a patron saint and day for the celebration of each saint. For instance, on September 24 León celebrates its saint *La Merced* ("Our Lady of Mercy"). It is a time to attend mass, but it is also a time for parties, processions, and carnivals. Carnival rides are moved to the main plaza, and young people get to stay up late eating, dancing, and going on rides. The image of La Merced is carried through the streets during the procession. It takes many men to carry the huge, heavy image. The city's streets are packed with people.

One part of the festival is more dangerous than most. A man wears a wood and paper frame built to look like a bull's upper body. The frame is wired with flares, rockets, and firecrackers. When the man lights the fuse, he runs straight into the crowd as his firecrackers shoot off in all directions. The people in León scream out of excitement and fear.

On November 1 Nicaraguans observe All Saints' Day, which honors the saints in the Catholic church. The next day, All Souls' Day, is a time for Catholics to remember the dead. The week before All Souls' Day is spent cleaning up the graveyard. Nicaraguans go to the graveyard to cut weeds and place flowers on the family grave. When All Souls' Day arrives, families take picnics to the graveyard and eat by the graves of their family members. They also take things that were special to the dead person, such as a hat or bottle of rum, and lay them out on the grave. After eating their picnic, people walk around the graveyard and visit with other families.

Although it isn't a Catholic holiday, Mother's Day is celebrated by all Nicaraguans. On this day children try to visit their mother. If they have enough money, people take their mother out for lunch or make a big dinner at home. Mothers are given gifts of perfume and jewelry. They may even be serenaded by visiting musicians in the early morning or late at night.

Celebrating Independence

Nicaraguans have many holidays honoring their country. In June and July there are official holidays every week in honor of the martyrs, or national heroes, who died in the revolution. There are also holidays in honor of the Sandinista revolution and the new Nicaraguan government. There are far too many holidays to celebrate all of them. People who like the Sandinista party try to go to as many events as they can.

The anniversary of the triumph of the revolution, when the Sandinistas defeated the Somoza government, takes place on July 19. Daniel Ortega and other Sandinista officials speak at a huge rally in Managua. Buses from all over Nicaragua take people to Managua for this big event.

An older national holiday is Independence Day—the day the Central American countries became independent from Spain. Independence Day, which is observed on September 15, is a holiday celebrated with much tradition in the city of Granada. Cherry bombs and firecrackers go off at six o'clock in the morning, reminding everyone that it's a national holiday. People

Young people marching in the Independence Day parade in Granada fill the city's central plaza.

gather at the central plaza early in the morning to wait for the parade. Schoolchildren stop in the plaza to have their black shoes shined and then go to school to line up for the parade. It seems like a long wait, but the parade finally begins. Small schoolchildren and high school drum and bugle corps members march through the streets to the plaza. The young people marching in the parade fill the area beside the plaza and wait to hear speeches by local government officials.

At a birthday party in León, Roxana swings a brightly decorated stick in an attempt to break the piñata that hangs above her.

Birthdays

The holiday that most children look forward to is one that is not tied to either the Catholic church or Nicaraguan history—their birthday. Birthdays mean that everyone gets dressed up in his or her best dress or shirt, wraps a small gift, and goes to the party hoping to break the piñata. Lunch is served first. Then the piñata, a papier-mâché figure filled with candy and small toys, is lowered from the ceiling. Each child is given a chance to strike at the piñata with a stick. It's not easy to break. The child with the stick is blindfolded, and before striking at the piñata, must dance to the music on the stereo or radio. Everyone shouts *"Baile, baile,"* which means "Dance, dance." Then an adult pulls a string that moves the piñata up and down while the child is striking at it. Once it breaks there is a mad dash for the candy.

Throughout the year, from Christmastime and Easter to Independence Day and Purísima, Nicaraguans celebrate religious and national holidays. For young people, these celebrations and others such as birthdays are times for fun, food, and a shared sense of family and community.

6. Families, Machismo, and "Painted Rooster"

Before the sun rises and before people get out of bed in the morning, roosters begin to crow across the country-side in Nicaragua. In her Managua neighborhood, Carmen hears the roosters and rolls over in bed for another hour of sleep. At 5:30 she wakes up again and gets up to start her work on this sunny day in September 1985.

Carmen's Family

Carmen turns on the radio and listens to the early morning news while she makes breakfast for her family. The noise from the radio, along with the banging of pots in the kitchen, wakens Carmen's family. They take turns showering, and then come to the table for a *desayuno* ("breakfast") of tortillas, *gallo pinto*, and cheese. Tortillas are flat and round and made of corn. Carmen buys them from a neighbor instead of making them because she doesn't have a wood stove to cook them properly. Carmen cooks with a two-burner electric hot pad. She warms the tortillas on one burner while she cooks gallo pinto on the other burner.

Gallo pinto, which means "painted rooster," is one of the most common Nicaraguan dishes. It is made of

A Nicaraguan family in Managua.

rice and red beans. The dish was given the name "painted rooster" because of the red and white colors of the beans and rice.

This breakfast is a favorite of Leyda, Carmen's fourteen-year-old daughter. Carmen's five-year-old granddaughter, Clarissa, has to be reminded to eat all of her breakfast. She is never hungry in the morning.

Clarissa lives with her grandmother because her mother, who lives in another part of Managua, is busy studying and working.

In Nicaragua grandmothers often raise their grandchildren. Many girls have babies when they are thirteen or fourteen years old. They seldom live with the father of the child. Instead, they live at home and work or go to school while their mother cares for the child. Sometimes they move away in search of work, leaving their child with their mother because they don't have enough money to care for the child.

Most families are not made up of just a mother, father, and children. Large, extended families usually share a home in Nicaragua. An extended family is one that might include a *tío* ("uncle"), *tía* ("aunt"), and *abuela* ("grandmother"). Carmen, her daughter Leyda, her granddaughter Clarissa, her daughter-in-law Rosa, and Rosa's baby Maria all live in Carmen's house. When he's home on leave from the army, Carmen's son Salvador also lives with his mother. Carmen's husband Jorge stays in Managua only on the weekends. He works at a factory in the northern city of Estelí during the week. Good jobs are hard to find in Managua, partly because the contra war has been hard on business, and partly because so many people move to Managua every day in search of work. As a result, Jorge must travel every week to his job in Estelí.

A Nicaraguan husband, wife, and child. Sadly, many Nicaraguan men abandon their families, leaving the mothers to raise the children alone.

Men, Machismo, and Marriage

Jorge supports his family, but many Nicaraguan women must raise their families on their own. Fathers often abandon their families and don't send money to help pay for food and clothing. Though the government is trying to force fathers to pay child support, it is impossible to locate all of the fathers who have left their children.

There are Nicaraguan men who are good fathers and husbands and treat women as their equals. Men's and women's roles are changing, but Nicaragua has a long tradition of *machismo*. Machismo is an attitude that most Nicaraguan men have. Men think they are superior to women and sometimes treat women badly. They love their mothers very much because they realize how hard their mothers had to work when they were young boys. Yet when men are with women who are their girl friends or wives, they don't treat them with the same respect they have for their mothers. It's an old problem that many people are trying to change, but it will take many years to change this attitude in men.

More Nicaraguans have common law marriages than official marriages. Common law marriage, which is accepted throughout Nicaragua, is a marriage that has never been made official with the church or government. It is a marriage that is recognized because a couple has lived together and has children together.

Sometimes, even though a couple would like to live together, it just isn't possible. Since Carmen's husband Jorge has to work in Estelí, Jorge and Carmen have no choice but to live apart during the week. Many other Nicaraguans, especially those who live in Managua, have to travel long distances to get to their jobs.

To the Market

After breakfast Carmen walks to *Mercado Eduardo Contreras* ("Eduardo Contreras Market") and shops for food. Many people ride the bus to the market. Since the buses are always crowded, Carmen prefers to walk. She knows several shortcuts to the market. One route takes her though a very poor *barrio*, or neighborhood. The people here live in tiny houses made out of tin, which don't have electricity or running water. Since the revolution, though, the streets in this neighborhood have been paved. The government plans to do much more in poor neighborhoods, but military spending has held back such plans. Another route to the market winds through a neighborhood where people have more money than Carmen's family. The people here live in bigger houses, and many of them own cars.

At the market Carmen goes directly to the section where food is sold. The market is huge and mostly indoors, separated into the clothing section and the food section. It was built by the government since the revolution. Not all markets in Nicaragua are so nice, though. Many of them are old and have no roof overhead.

If she wanted, Carmen could shop at a supermarket. She prefers the produce at the market because she thinks it's fresher. In the string bag she carries with

People buy fresh food at a busy market in Managua.

her, Carmen puts *tomates* ("tomatoes"), *queso* ("cheese"), *pan* ("bread"), *repollo* ("cabbage"), and *naranjas* ("oranges"). She buys each item from a different vendor, or seller. The market is filled with stalls where people sell their products. Since the bright colors of the fruits and vegetables and flowers show up from far away, Carmen can easily see the foods she wants to purchase.

Carmen asks how much each item costs before buying it. If she feels that something is too expensive, she either walks on to another vendor or stays to bargain over the price. She barters if she thinks the vendor will eventually offer her a lower price. Carmen and the vendor bargain over the price until they are both satisfied.

Lunchtime and House Cleaning

When Carmen gets home, she makes *almuerzo* ("lunch"). Lunch is chicken soup, white bread with a thick crust, and cheese. By noon it's hot outside, so Leyda and Clarissa drink several glasses of *refresco* ("cold drink"). Because of the heat, cold drinks are one of the favorite foods served at lunch. Refresco is fruit juice with sugar added to make it sweet. It is made in every color imaginable since there are so many kinds of fruit in Nicaragua. *Pintalla* is magenta, a bright pink-purple. *Tamarindo* ("tamarind") is brown, and *mango* ("mango") is yellow.

Because drinking glasses are hard to find, many people use cut-off soda pop bottles with dulled edges for glasses. A thick drink of corn powder and chocolate is often served in hollow gourds. The gourds are carved and the ends cut off. They work something like a thermos, keeping liquids cold even without ice.

Most refrescos and *gaseosa* ("soda pop") bought from a street vendor come in plastic bags. The vendor pours the drink into a small plastic bag, adds crushed ice, ties a knot in the bag, and shakes the bag until the drink is cold. Then the buyer bites a small corner out of the bag and holds the bag with both hands while drinking. It sounds very tricky, but Nicaraguans who ride the bus from town to town are used to drinking this way. They can drink out of plastic bags while standing in the aisle of a crowded, bumpy bus and not spill a drop!

On their way to school on hot days, Leyda and Clarissa sometimes stop and buy a cold drink. They go to school during the afternoon shift, which is the hottest time of the day. Rosa, Carmen's daughter-in-law, works at a factory in the evening. For a few late afternoon hours, then, Carmen and her granddaughter Maria are the only ones at home.

While Maria takes a nap, Carmen washes clothes and cleans the house. She washes clothes by hand in the kitchen sink. She rubs them hard on a washboard with soap, rinses them, and hangs them on the clothesline to dry. The clothes dry in a couple of hours in the afternoon sunshine.

Since the house isn't very big, it doesn't take Carmen long to clean the entire place. She sweeps the red tile floor in the living room first, then goes on to the kitchen, bathroom, and the four bedrooms, where the floors are cement. Two of the bedrooms have doors, and the other two have curtains separating them from the living room. The rooms are painted in bright pink and green, which makes them seem bright even though there isn't much sunlight. The only windows in the house face the street. The other sides of the house are common walls shared with the neighbors.

Carmen works quickly but carefully. While she works she thinks about her husband far away in Estelí and hopes he isn't too lonely. She thinks about her two sons in the army and worries about them fighting the contras near the Honduran border.

Suppertime and Neighborhood Visitors

When Carmen finishes cleaning, she makes *cena* ("supper"). Since she has a refrigerator, she can prepare meat more often than most Nicaraguans. When Leyda and Clarissa get home from school at six o'clock, they are tired and hungry. After a supper of fried fish, gallo pinto, and bread, they feel much better. Leyda helps her mother with the dishes, and then all three of them sit down in front of the television.

Almost all homes in the towns and cities of western Nicaragua have several rocking chairs. In the homes where there are televisions, the rocking chairs are often set in front of the TV set. The chairs come in two sizes:

A Nicaraguan girl does the family's dishes after a meal.

The neighborhood gang drops in for an evening visit.

small, for children, and large, for adults. They are made of cane and carved wood. Carmen and the girls rock and watch TV while they wait for Rosa to come home from work.

Evenings in Managua are filled with neighborhood activity. Everyone leaves the front door open so they can greet passers-by. Carmen says "*Hola, mi amor*" ("hello, my love") to the neighborhood children. Some stop by to watch television. Others—those who don't have a refrigerator—ask if they can buy ice. Carmen buys tortillas from a girl who walks by selling some she just made. An old woman who lives across the street comes to visit with Carmen. At 8:30 Carmen tells the girls it is time for them to go to bed. They say they aren't tired and ask if they can watch just one more TV show. Carmen insists, though, and they finally go to bed.

Nicaraguan Lifestyles

Children in other parts of Nicaragua are going to bed at the same time as Leyda and Clarissa. If they are from a poor family, they probably sleep in a *jamaca* ("hammock") or a *tijera* ("cot"). Some poor children don't go to school regularly because they have to earn money for their family. If the children live in a city, they might work as vendors, selling newspapers or refrescos, or they might shine shoes. If they live in a rural area, they are more likely to work with their parents in the fields.

Children from wealthy families don't have to work around the house. These families have a *doméstica* ("maid") who cleans and washes clothes, another maid who cooks, and a third maid who cares for the children. They live in beautiful homes and sometimes take vacations in the United States and in other countries.

Although the lifestyles vary one from another, a few things are common to most Nicaraguan homes. Throughout the country, families have a set of wooden rocking chairs. And whether the maid or mother does the cooking, she probably serves gallo pinto at least once a day. You can learn to make gallo pinto, too, by following the recipe given below. There are also recipes for a couple of other Nicaraguan foods to try out on your family and friends. If they like your cooking, they should tell you it's *"bien rico"* ("very delicious").

Gallo Pinto ("Painted Rooster")

1 tablespoon vegetable oil
1/2 medium onion, chopped fine
1 cup white rice, cooked
1 cup red beans, cooked
optional: bottle hot pepper sauce (a few drops)

Put 1 tablespoon oil in frying pan. Cook the onion in the hot oil, turning until brown. Add the rice and beans and cook for five to ten minutes, stirring constantly. Add a few drops of bottled hot sauce if you like, then fry the mixture until the oil is gone and the rice and beans are crisp. Makes 4 servings.

Banana con Leche ("Banana Milkshake")

1/3 cup powdered sugar
2 large ripe bananas
2 cups milk
1 teaspoon vanilla
Ice

Put all ingredients except ice in blender. Blend until mixed thoroughly. Put ice in glasses and fill the glasses with the milkshake. Makes 2 servings.

Quesillos ("Cheesies")

1/4 pound moist white cheese, cubed
4 soft-shell corn tortillas
Bottled taco sauce

Warm tortillas in the microwave or oven. Place cubed cheese on top of heated tortilla. Pour a little taco sauce on top of the cheese, then fold the tortilla in half. Makes 4 servings.

7. *A Right to an Education*

Young and old alike are students in Nicaragua. In 1986 the Nicaraguan ministry of education reported that one-third of the people in the country were students. Grade school students ride school buses in the morning and afternoon. City buses carry university and adult education students home from evening class.

The government believes that all Nicaraguans have a right to an education. Before the revolution in 1979, most people had a difficult time getting an education. Schools weren't built in remote mountain areas. Children often helped their parents with the work at home instead of attending school. Anastasio "Tachito" Somoza didn't spend much money on education, and he banned many books that he thought would give people ideas about their rights.

Today the contra war makes it difficult for schools to educate students. Schools in the war zone are sometimes attacked, and the government has less money to spend on education as it spends more to defend Nicaragua against the contras. In 1981 the government could give the country one new classroom per week. By 1986 the government had almost no money available to build new classrooms.

During the early 1980s, the Nicaraguan government built many new schools like this one.

A Nicaraguan School Day

In spite of the problems, children all over Nicaragua go to school. On a September morning in 1985, students in León line up at 6:45 to wait for their school bus. Almost all of the girls wear white blouses and dark skirts. The boys wear white shirts and dark pants. Boys carry their books in a backpack, while girls carry their books in a book bag. Some students carry their desks to and from school on their heads so they won't get stolen overnight. The old school bus, painted white with red trim, drops the students off at school and goes to pick up another bus load. Since buses are one of many shortages in Nicaragua, often a bus must cover two routes before school starts. Until the second load arrives, students play in the school yard.

When the bell rings, the students run to class. Professor López, called "*Profe*" by the students, takes roll. All but two of the thirty-eight students in the fourth grade are present. The first class of the day is *agropecuario*, which is about tools and gardening as well as agricultural crops such as cotton and coffee. The government wants Nicaraguans to understand gardening and to raise gardens at home. It also wants schoolchildren to become interested in Nicaraguan agriculture because the country needs farmers to raise enough food for the people. Professor López gives a *dictado*, a quiz read out loud. She asks how far apart carrots should be planted, how carrots are harvested, and what time of the year cotton is harvested. Students write out the answers, and then hand in their papers.

Professor López returns tests in math class. She reads the percentage grades out loud as she returns them. Then she writes the percentage grades next to the letter grades on the blackboard, which makes some students groan and others sigh with relief.

By mid-morning the classroom gets warm. This school, like most in Nicaragua, has walls made of cement blocks. The cement blocks have holes in them that allow the outside air to move through the school. Sometimes the walls rise just halfway to the roof. When a breeze blows through the room, the fresh air feels good, but everyone has to hold on to their papers! The walls don't keep out all of the noise from neighboring classrooms, either. Students have to learn to concentrate and not be distracted by a discussion next door.

In Spanish class the fourth graders read a play. For them it is more interesting than the spelling unit they just finished. The play has new words that they are supposed to learn before their vocabulary test the following week.

Next it's time for physical education, a favorite class for many young people. Those who have gym clothes change into shorts and T-shirts. Boys and girls are separated during physical education. The girls play basketball on an outdoor court, and the boys play soccer.

While the fourth graders have physical education, children from other grades clean up around the school yard. The sixth graders shovel the mud so that water will run out of the puddles. Mosquitoes carrying a disease called *dengue* breed in water puddles. If the puddles are drained, the mosquitoes can't breed there.

Students clean up a school yard in León.

The kindergarten class washes the lunch tables. The third graders pick up litter that has been thrown on the school yard. All students in Nicaragua are expected to help with these chores a few times a week.

When Professor López returns for the last class of the day, the assignment is to read a section in the science book. Since the book has too many pages to finish in class, it must be finished at home. The bell rings at noon, and school is done for the day. While they wait for their buses, some students buy snacks from the women selling them by the school gate. One of the favorites is a snack made of a vegetable called yucca, crackers, cabbage, and fried pig skin, all shredded into small pieces and served on banana leaves. It's eaten with the fingers.

Split-Shifts and Final Exams

Nicaraguan schools run on a split-shift schedule because there aren't enough schools, teachers, and buses for every student to have a full day of school. Some students attend the morning shift, while others attend the afternoon shift. Each shift is five hours long.

There are public and private schools in Nicaragua. In the public schools the government pays teachers, and parents don't pay tuition for their children. In private schools, most of which are run by the Catholic church, parents pay for the classes their children take.

At the end of the school year all Nicaraguan students, from public and private schools, have to take final exams. They are tested in math, Spanish, social science, and natural science. Since the tests are held the first week in December, students all over Nicaragua study hard in late November. The tests are taken seriously. If students fail two or three parts of the exam,

In a neighborhood of Managua, young people study for school.

they may repeat the exam. If they fail all four parts, they must repeat the grade.

The school year in Nicaragua runs from April to mid-December. Sometimes students—especially older students—can complete two grades in one year. Many students fifteen years old and older are just now completing primary school. The revolution made it difficult for them to attend school regularly during the late 1970s.

Education for Everyone

For those who cannot attend school during the day, the government offers night classes. Adults attending school often take night classes. Many older Nicaraguans have recently learned to read and write—something they never had a chance to do when they were young.

Eight months after the Sandinistas won the revolution in 1979, they held a literacy campaign to teach people to read. Before the campaign, just over half of the population over the age of ten could read and write. The literacy campaign enlisted Nicaraguans who were at least twelve years old and had received at least a full primary education. They were taught how to teach and were sent to every corner of Nicaragua to share their skills. Many teachers from the city experienced rural life for the first time during this campaign.

Although the campaign suffered setbacks from time to time, most of the goals were met. UNESCO— the United Nations Educational, Scientific, and Cultural Organization—awarded the Nicaraguan government the 1980 grand prize in literacy. UNESCO called the literacy campaign "the most important movement in this generation." Many Nicaraguans who learned to read and write during the campaign now teach others.

The ministry of education encourages education for people of all ages. The Sandinistas believe that the ability to read and write gives people power they have never had. They want to educate Nicaraguans so they can read newspapers and think about the world around them as well as their own community.

Nicaragua needs and continues to train more teachers. It is also training many doctors, nurses, and agronomists—scientists who study field crops. These professions require many years of education. There are universities in Estelí, León, Managua, Matagalpa, Rivas, and Granada. Not all universities offer all degrees. For instance, someone who wants to become a dentist must study at the university in León. Students studying to become doctors attend the university in León or Managua.

After primary school most students have three years of general studies. Some students choose to attend a vocational-technical school. Not all continue their

The Children's Library in Managua has brightly painted murals to attract young people to the books inside.

education after primary school. Many get a job without further schooling.

It may be a long time before Nicaraguans have the schools and books they need. For the time being, teachers and students manage to keep the classes going even though there are many shortages and difficulties to overcome. They are working together so that all Nicaraguans have the chance to get an education.

8. Baseball, Homemade Toys, and Videos

Some of the favorite Nicaraguan pastimes began in that part of the world hundreds of years ago. Others had their origin in Spain or the United States. Bullfighting came from Spain, while baseball is a pastime Nicaragua and the United States share. Nicaraguans consider baseball to be one of the good things they received from the United States.

Baseball and Frozen Tag

Baseball is the number one sport in Nicaragua. Boys look forward to playing *beis* whenever they have some free time. They play on a baseball field if there's one nearby. If they don't have a field, they play in empty lots or side streets. Their heroes are David Green, Al Williams, and Dennis Martínez—Nicaraguans who have played in *Las Ligas Grandes* ("The Big Leagues") in the United States.

Though some boys are lucky enough to have standard baseball equipment, most have to use whatever is available. Often tennis balls or taped rags take the place of a ball. The batter uses either a stick or his forearm for a bat. To bat with his forearm, he throws the ball up in

Boys play Nicaragua's number one sport on a baseball field in León.

the air and hits it with his arm when it comes down. That way no one needs to pitch.

Besides baseball, other sports and games are popular with Nicaraguan young people. Girls are more likely to play basketball or softball, and boys also play basketball and soccer. Another popular game, frozen tag, is called *el perro congelado* which means "the frozen dog." In frozen tag, the person who is "it" freezes the person she catches. That person must stand frozen in one spot until he is freed by other players who have not yet been caught.

Pets, Toys, and Games

Many children have dogs or cats for pets. When he comes home from school in León, ten-year-old José Antonio plays with his little white dog. He also plays with his *trompa*, which is a small wooden top with a string. The string is wound around the top until José Antonio uses it to make the top spin. Nicaraguans say that a top *baila* ("dances") instead of "spins." Because he has had many hours of practice, José Antonio can get the top to "dance" on an uneven rock or in a crack in the floor.

A *bolero* is another toy made of wood and string. A wooden cup with a handle has a small wooden ball attached to it with a string. The purpose of this toy is to try to catch the ball in the cup.

Toys and games are hard for most people to find in stores or to afford if they do find them. Nicaraguan children are skilled at making games and toys. For instance, they may paint a checkerboard on a sidewalk or steps and use bottle caps for checkers. Or they may play jacks with small stones. Kites are made out of

Nicaraguan girls and boys have fun playing games together and even make their own equipment and toys.

paper and bent clothes hangers. Toys can be fashioned out of machine parts and just about anything else you can imagine.

Many activities in Nicaragua are for both children and adults. If they live close to a beach, families sometimes take a picnic lunch to the seashore where they enjoy swimming or wading in the water. Wealthy families may take a longer vacation, perhaps in a foreign country. Most Nicaraguans travel inside their country, often to visit friends and relatives.

Nicaraguan TV and Movies

Watching TV and visiting with neighbors is a common way for city people to spend evenings. Though there are just two TV stations in Nicaragua, they carry programs from all over the world. Music videos are especially popular with young people. Young children watch Mickey Mouse and Yogi the Bear cartoons from the United States. A Cuban comedy called "*Las Impuras*" ("The Impure Ones") is televised in the evening. "Ronda of Piedra," a Brazilian soap opera, has faithful followers in many Nicaraguan homes.

Some sports events are televised. Though Nicaragua has no professional teams, it does have organized teams for skilled players of many sports—baseball, soccer, basketball, boxing, weight lifting, volleyball, softball, judo, karate, swimming, track, and fencing. When there are tournaments with all of the Central American teams, sports fans go to a stadium to see them in person or watch them on television.

Movies are a popular pastime in Nicaraguan cities. The lines at theaters get very long if the movie is a good one. When *Breakdance* was showing in Managua in the fall of 1985 some kids broke the windows of the theater because they were so eager to get in to see it.

Las corridas de toros ("bullfights") are held during festivals. In Nicaragua the bulls aren't killed at the end

Nicaraguans wait in line to see a popular movie in Managua.

of the bullfight, but they are teased with a red cape just as in Spain and Mexico.

A National Corn Fair

Some forms of Nicaraguan recreation serve more than one purpose. In the early 1980s, the ministry of culture held a corn fair. One purpose of the fair was to help people have a good time. The other purpose was to

encourage pride in the Nicaraguan tradition of cooking with corn. The corn fair was held at a time when people had to rely on corn rather than wheat because the United States wasn't sending wheat to Nicaragua. The slogan of the fair was *Maíz, Nuestra Raíz*, which rhymes in Spanish. In English it means, "Corn, Our Roots."

The fair was celebrated in all parts of the country. Then a national contest was held in the Indian town of Monimbó. Contests were held for various dishes made out of corn. Judges tasted tortillas, tamales (a corn dough wrapped in leaves and eaten with cheese), *Indio Viejo* ("Old Indian," an Indian corn stew), *cosas-de-horno* ("things from the oven," various baked goods), *pinol* (the national drink, made from corn flour with water), and *chicha* ("corn wine").

Most festivals are held in the plaza or marketplace of a city or town. The plaza and market are usually near the center of town and are common meeting places for people. From a park bench in the central plaza, a person can keep track of much downtown activity.

The Nicaraguan government is building more places for people to go in their free time. Parks and zoos are being constructed for city people. Since most Nicaraguans in the city have no yards, they like to get away to a place that's green and shaded. A park and zoo are being developed on the edge of León. They are called

Arlen Siu, the name of a child who died in the revolution. A children's park in downtown Managua is named for Luis Alfonso Velásquez, another child who died in the revolution. Children play basketball and baseball in this park every day.

Whether they are playing baseball, making homemade toys, listening to music videos, or spending time at the beach or in a park, Nicaraguans find ways to relax and have fun. Poor and rich alike, they enjoy their sports, games, and forms of recreation.

9. A Love for Their Homeland

Nicaraguans have come to the United States for a variety of reasons. Some Americans of Nicaraguan heritage have lived here all their lives. Their parents or grandparents moved here many years ago. But most Nicaraguans living in the United States have come here recently. They have come because of the revolution, and later, the contra war in their homeland.

It is impossible to know exactly how many Nicaraguans live in the United States. Since most have come without legal permission, they aren't listed in any U.S. government records. Immigration officials estimate that 100,000 Nicaraguans live in the United States.

Some Nicaraguans fled north before July 1979 because they were afraid they would be killed by Somoza's National Guard or caught in the crossfire between the Sandinistas and the government army. Other Nicaraguans left because they were friends of Somoza and were afraid of losing their wealth and privileges if the Sandinistas came to power.

Since 1979 a number of well-to-do Nicaraguans have left their country because they don't agree with the Sandinistas. Others have left because their homes and villages became contra war zones. In some cases entire families have moved to the United States because they opposed Somoza when he was in power. Now they oppose the Sandinistas, and they don't plan to return to Nicaragua unless the current government is removed from power.

The largest group of Nicaraguans in the United States lives in Miami, Florida. U.S. officials estimate that 45,000 Nicaraguans live in Miami—almost half of the Nicaraguans in the United States. A large number of these people are wealthy, and many have expensive homes in Miami and Nicaragua. In some cases they left Nicaragua because land they owned was given to poor, landless peasants since the Sandinista government came to power. Some Nicaraguan business people left because they believed they would have to pay such high taxes that their business would lose money.

Many of these wealthy Nicaraguans support the contras. They send money and supplies to the contras to support their war against the Sandinistas. They want to return to Nicaragua when the Sandinistas are no longer governing the country.

The Edgar Chamorro Story

Edgar Chamorro is a Nicaraguan who once supported the contras. In fact, after he and his family moved to Miami in 1979, he was a director of the FDN,

Edgar Chamorro was once one of the civilian directors of the FDN, the largest contra organization.

the largest contra organization, for two years. Chamorro has a privileged background. He was a Roman Catholic priest and has several university degrees. When he left the priesthood in 1969, he started both an educational consulting firm and an advertising agency in Managua. In 1977 he spent a year in New York as a member of the mission of Nicaragua to the United States.

He returned to Nicaragua, but during the civil war moved with his wife and children to Miami. Once in the United States, he began to work with other Nicaraguans who opposed the new Nicaraguan government. Chamorro eventually became one of the civilian directors of the FDN. He left the FDN in 1984 after he became a critic of the actions of the contras. In recent years Chamorro has written several articles criticizing the policy of the U.S. government and calling for a political instead of military solution to the conflict in Nicaragua.

Asylum in the United States

In order to live legally in the United States, Nicaraguans like Chamorro must apply for asylum, or official permission, from the U.S. government. In the past the U.S. government has often treated Nicaraguans as economic refugees. It claimed that Nicaraguans were seeking refuge, or shelter, in order to make more money than they could in Nicaragua. Today the U.S. government is more likely to consider Nicaraguans to be political refugees.

U.S. officials are most likely to grant asylum to Nicaraguans they believe are mistreated by the Nicaraguan government or those who are in danger because they live along the Honduran border where fighting takes place. Nicaraguans who are granted asylum may be Miskito Indians or priests and pastors who speak out against their government. These groups of Nicaraguans, the U.S. government believes, have been treated badly by the Sandinistas. Nicaraguans who have lived in the United States for a long time usually have a more difficult time getting legal permission to stay. Young men who don't want to serve in the Nicaraguan army are not routinely granted asylum either.

The U.S. Immigration and Naturalization Service director in Florida has said that he will not send back Nicaraguans to their native land because he is concerned they might be harmed by the Nicaraguan government. Federal officials say that at least three-fourths of all asylum applications by Nicaraguans come from Florida.

Nicaraguan Refugees

Not all Nicaraguans in the United States live in Florida, and not all of them are wealthy. Poor Nicaraguans who leave their country often arrive in the United States on foot. Some never make it as far as the United States. They may end up in refugee camps in Honduras, where living conditions are difficult. The Honduran army guards the camps, and the people who live in them are not free to come and go as they please. Other refugees travel as far as Mexico, sometimes living in camps set up for refugees, and sometimes working in restaurants or factories.

If they want to get as far north as the United States, poor Nicaraguans may hire guides called "coyotes" who will take them across the border between Mexico and the United States. Not everyone makes it across the border without getting caught. U.S. immigration officials who patrol the border catch many refugees trying to slip across it.

Some refugees who manage to cross the border apply for asylum. These people are often called "illegal aliens" because they don't have legal papers that give them permission to live in the United States. Until recently, *Casa Oscar Romero* ("Oscar Romero House") in San Benito, Texas, housed some Central American refugees who had no other place to go. The four-room house, which was run by a Catholic sister, had more than 500 refugees staying there at one time.

At Casa Oscar Romero and other places like it throughout the U.S. South and Southwest, refugees are taught certain skills that they will need to get along in this new and foreign country. Sometimes Nicaraguans are able to take English classes. In other cases, places like Casa Oscar Romero help refugees find jobs.

Refugees who move on to Houston or Miami or Los Angeles may have relatives waiting for them. These

Nicaraguan refugee children stand in front of Casa Oscar Romero in San Benito, Texas.

cities have large numbers of Spanish-speaking people from Mexico and Central America. The lifestyle in these Hispanic communities is usually quite similar to the lifestyle in those Latin American nations. There are Spanish television and radio stations, Spanish newspapers, and rice, beans, and tortillas to eat.

In spite of these familiar things, life away from home can be lonely for refugees. They have family and friends still living in Nicaragua. They worry about getting a job in the United States and keeping it once they get one. It is against the law for employers to hire illegal aliens. Many employers, such as truck farmers and restaurant and factory managers, hire illegal aliens because they will work for less money than U.S. citizens. Even after they have a job, refugees worry about getting caught by immigration officials and sent back to Nicaragua.

Bianca Jagger is a well-known Nicaraguan who works to help poor Nicaraguans. Although her home is now in London, she spends a great deal of time in the United States. She speaks out in defense of her native country and against the contra war.

Bianca Perez Morena de Macias was born to a wealthy Nicaraguan family. She left Nicaragua in 1964 and began a career as a model. In 1971 she married rock star Mick Jagger of the Rolling Stones and joined the jet-set in London and New York. She persuaded the Rolling Stones to stage a benefit concert for Nicaraguan earthquake victims in 1973. Jagger divorced her husband in 1979.

In recent years Jagger has testified before the U.S. Congress and filed reports with international rights organizations. She says it is "my duty to monitor the situation and speak out" about Nicaragua and other Central American countries. Jagger has given her time and money to support the Nicaraguan health and education campaigns.

Four other well-known Nicaraguans in the United

States have at least one thing in common: they are baseball players. Dennis Martínez plays for the Baltimore Orioles. Al Williams pitched for the Minnesota Twins at one time and now plays in the minor leagues. Porfirio Altamirano plays for the New York Yankees, and David Green also plays professional baseball. Many excellent baseball players have come from this small country.

Nicaraguans in the United States are divided in several ways. Some are rich; others are poor. Many support the contras; a great number defend the Sandinistas. What they have in common is a love for their homeland. And, like people everywhere, they want peace.

Appendix A

Nicaraguan Consulates in the United States and Canada

Nicaraguan consulates in the United States and Canada offer assistance to Americans and Canadians who want to understand Nicaraguan ways. For information and resource materials about Nicaragua, contact the consulate or embassy nearest you.

U.S. Consulate and Embassy

Washington, D.C.
   Nicaraguan Embassy
   1627 New Hampshire Avenue N.W.
   Washington, DC 20009
   Phone (202) 387-4371

Washington, D.C.
   Consulate General of Nicaragua
   1627 New Hampshire Avenue N.W.
   Washington, DC 20009
   Phone (202) 387-4371

Canadian Consulate and Embassy

Ottawa, Ontario
   Nicaraguan Embassy
   170 Laurier Avenue West
   Ottawa, Ontario K1P 5V5
   Phone (613) 234-9361

Ottawa, Ontario
   Consulate General of Nicaragua
   4 Topaz Gate
   Willowdale, Ontario M2M 2Z7
   Phone (416) 221-3092

Appendix B
Say It in Spanish!

English Word(s)	Spanish Word(s)	Pronunciation
hello	hola	(OH·lah)
good-bye	adiós	(ah·DEEOHS)
yes	sí	(SEE)
no	no	(NOH)
good morning	buenas días	(BWAY·nahs DEE·ahs)
good night	buenas noches	(BWAY·nahs NOH·chays)
thank you	gracias	(GRAH·seeahs)
please	por favor	(POHR fah·VOHR)
excuse me	perdóneme	(pehr·DOH·nay·may)
what do you want?	¿qué quieres?	(kay·kee·AI·rays)
how are you?	¿cómo estás?	(koh·moh·ehs·TAHS)
Mr.	Señor	(seh·NYOHR)
Mrs.	Señora	(seh·NYOHR·ah)
Miss	Señorita	(seh·nyohr·EE·tah)
Ms.	Seña	(SEH·nyah)

Spanish Adjectives

English Word(s)	Masculine Form	Feminine Form
good	bueno (BWAY·noh)	buena (BWAY·nah)
bad	malo (MAH·loh)	mala (MAH·lah)
pretty	bonito (boh·NEE·toh)	bonita (boh·NEE·tah)
ugly	feo (FAY·oh)	fea (FAY·ah)
big	grande (GRAHN·day)	grande (GRAHN·day)
small	pequeño (pay·KAY·nyoh)	pequeña (pay·KAY·nyah)

Glossary

abajo (ah·BAH·hoh)—down

abrazos de paz (ah·BRAH·sohs day PAHS)—hugs of peace, exchanged among friends and family on Christmas Eve

abuela (ah·BWAY·lah)—grandmother

adiós (ah·dee·OHS)—good-bye

agropecuario (ah·groh·peh·koo·AH·ree·oh)—agronomy; a class about gardening and agriculture

almuerzo (ahl·MWAIR·soh)—lunch

arriba (ah·REE·bah)—up

Azul (ah·SOOL)—a collection of writing by Rubén Darío

baile (BY·lay)—dance

banana con leche (bah·NAH·nah kohn LAY· chay)—banana milkshake

beis (BAYS)—the game of baseball

bien rico (beeehn REE·koh)—very delicious

bolero (boh·LAY·roh)—a toy made of wood and string

Cantos de Vida y Esperanza (KAHN·tohs day VEE·dah EE ehs·pai·RAHN·sah)—*Songs of Life and Hope*, a book written by Rubén Darío

Casa Oscar Romero (KAH·sah OHS·kahr roh·may·roh)—a house in San Benito, Texas, which shelters Central American refugees

cena (SAY·nah)—supper

chicha (CHEE·chah)—corn liquor

chozas (CHOH·sahs)—houses made of tree branches

contras (KOHN·trahs)—counterrevolutionaries; a group of soldiers fighting to overthrow the Sandinista government

Las corridas de toros (lahs koh·REE·dahs day TOH·rohs)—bullfights

cosas-de-horno (KOH·sahs day OHR·noh)—"things from the oven," various baked goods

Costa Atlántica (KOHS·tah aht·LAHN·tee·kah)—Atlantic Coast

¿Cuántos años tiene? (KWAHN·tohs AHN·yohs tee EH·nay)—How old are you?

dengue (DEHN·gay)—a disease carried by mosquitoes

desayuno (day·say·OO·noh)—breakfast

Las Doce (lahs DOH·say)—"The Twelve," a group of twelve men who demanded that Somoza step down from power

doméstica (doh·MEHS·tee·kah)—maid

exteriorismo (ehs·tayr·ee·oh·REES·moh)—a movement in poetry that reflects the real things around us every day

fresco (FREHS·koh)—fresh; nice and cool

gallo pinto (GY·oh PEEN·toh)—"painted rooster," a dish made of rice and red beans

gaseosa (gah·say·OH·sah)—soda pop

la Gigantona (lah hee·gahn·TOH·nah)—the Giant, a giant puppet

Gran Lago (gran LAH·goh)—Great Lake, a nickname for Lake Nicaragua

la gritería (lah gree·tay·REE·ah)—"the shouting;" a part of the Purísima celebration when people walk from house to house shouting that they are happy because of the immaculate conception of Mary

los hermanitos de la costa (lohs air·mah·NEE·tohs day lah KOH·stah)—"the little brothers of the coast," an expression sometimes used by people in western Nicaragua to describe the people of eastern Nicaragua

Hola (OH·lah)—"hello"

Hola, mi amor (OH·lah mee ah·MOHR)—"Hello, my love"

Las Impuras (lahs eem·POO·rahs)—"The Impure Ones," a Cuban television show

indio viejo (EEN·vee·oh bee·AY·hoh)—"Old Indian," an Indian corn stew

jamaca (hah·MAH·kah)—hammock

lago (LAH·goh)—lake

Las Ligas Grandes (lahs LEE·gahs GRAHN·days)—"the Big Leagues;" the professional U.S. baseball leagues

Loma de Tiscapa (LOH·mah day tees·KAH·pah)—Tiscapa Hill, a hill in Managua

Maíz, Nuestra Raíz (mah·EES noo·EHS·trah rah· EES)—"Corn, Our Roots," the slogan for a corn fair held in Nicaragua

mango (MAHN·goh)—mango, a yellow fruit

Mercado Eduardo Contreras (mayr·KAH·doh ehd· WAHR·doh kohn·TRAY·rahs)—Eduardo Contreras Market, a new market in Managua

La Merced (LAH mayr·SAYD)—Our Lady of Mercy, the patron saint of León

mestizos (mehs·TEE·sohs)—people of mixed Spanish and Indian ancestry

montaña (mohn·TAHN·yah)—mountain

naranjas (nah·RAHN·hahs)—oranges

Navidad (nah·vee·DAHD)—Christmas

Nuestra Señora de Solentiname (noo·EHS·trah seh· NYOHR·ah day soh·lehn·tee·NAH·may)—Our Lady of Solentiname, a community of artists on a group of islands in Lake Nicaragua

pan (PAHN)—bread

Pascua (PAHS·kwah)—Easter

el perro congelado (ehl PAY·rro kohn·hay·LAH·doh)— frozen tag; it means "the frozen dog"

piñata (pee·NYAH·tah)—a papier-mâché figure with candy inside, which children try to break at birthday parties

pinol (pee·NOHL)—the national drink in Nicaragua, made from corn flour and water

pintalla (peen·TAH·yah)—a magenta colored fruit

Poeta Cardenal (poh·AY·tah kahr·day·NAHL—Poet Cardenal, the Minister of Culture and a famous poet

La Prensa (lah PREHN·sah)—"The Press," the name of a well-known newspaper in Managua; it has recently been shut down by the government

Prosas Profanas (PROH·sahs proh·FAH·nahs)—*Profane Prose*, a book written by Rubén Darío

El Punche de Oro de los Subtiavas (ehl POON·chay day OH·roh day lohs soob·tee·AH·vahs)—The Gold Crab of the Subtiavas, a story from the community of Subtiava

Purísima (poor·EE·see·mah)—The Virgin Mary; a holiday celebrated on December 6 and 7 in Nicaragua

¿ Qué hora es? (kay oh·rah AYS)—What time is it?

quesillos (kay·SEE·yohs)—"cheesies," heated tortillas with cubes of cheese and hot sauce

queso (KAY·soh)—cheese

refresco (rray·FREHS·koh)—cold drink

repollo (rray·POH·yoh)—cabbage

Semana Santa (say·MAH·nah SAHN·tah)- "Holy Week," the week leading up to Easter

tamarindo (tah·mah·REEN·doh)—tamarind, a brown fruit

tía (TEE·ah)—aunt

tijera (tee·HAY·rah)—cot

tío (TEE·oh)—uncle
tomates (toh·MAH·tays)—tomatoes
Volcán Cerro Negro (vohl·KAHN SAY·rroh NAY·
groh)—Black Hill Volcano, a volcano near León

Selected Bibliography

An Americas Watch Report: Violations of the Laws of War by Both Sides in Nicaragua 1981-1985. New York: Americas Watch, March 1985.

Barry, Tom; Wood, Beth; and Preusch, Deb. *Dollars and Dictators: A Guide to Central America.* New York: Grove Press, 1983.

Black, George. *Triumph of the People: The Sandinista Revolution in Nicaragua.* London: Zed Press, 1981.

Brody, Reed. *Contra Terror in Nicaragua: Report of a Fact-finding Mission September 1984-January 1985.* Boston: South End Press, 1985.

"Central America: What U.S. Educators Need to Know." *Interracial Books for Children Bulletin.* Vol. 13, Nos. 2-3, New York: 1982.

Christian, Shirley. *Nicaragua: Revolution in the Family.* New York: Random House, 1985.

Collins, Joseph, with Moore Lappe, Frances; Allen, Nick; and Rice, Paul. *Nicaragua: What Difference Could a Revolution Make?* San Francisco: Food First, 1985.

Grossman, Karl. *Nicaragua: America's New Vietnam?* Sag Harbor, New York: The Permanent Press, 1984.

Hirshon, Sheryl, with Butler, Judy. *And Also Teach Them to Read.* Westport, Connecticut: Lawrence Hill & Company, 1983.

Lernoux, Penny. *Cry of the People: The Struggle for Human Rights in Latin America.* New York: Penguin Books, 1982.

Marcus, Bruce, ed. *Sandinistas Speak.* New York: Pathfinder Press, 1982.

Randall, Margaret. *Sandino's Daughters: Testimonies of Nicaraguan Women in Struggle.* Lynda Yanz, ed. Toronto: New Star Books, 1981.

Rosset, Peter, and Vandermeer, John, eds. *The Nicaragua Reader: Documents of a Revolution under Fire.* New York: Grove Press, 1983.

Volcán: Poems from El Salvador, Guatemala, Honduras, Nicaragua. San Francisco: City Lights Books, 1983.

Index

148

About the Author

A free-lance writer and the author of *El Salvador: Beauty Among the Ashes*, Faith Adams gathered firsthand information in Nicaragua in preparation for writing this book. Throughout the country, she visited schools, hospitals, and talked with local government officials. In some places she stayed with Nicaraguan families, and everywhere she found the people willing to open their homes and share their lives with her. Ms. Adams also conducted an independent study of *Amas de Casa*, a Central American women's organization. Her earlier experience in Central America led her to study and write about people in that part of the world.

Ms. Adams's educational background includes a bachelor's degree in English from Saint Olaf's College. She and her husband live in Minneapolis.